Jonathan reached for Olivia's free hand.

"Getting my own rig is my dream, even after what happened with Robby. Don't look at me like that. I'll say his name if I want to. You weren't the only one who lost someone."

"I know that." Her voice barely sounded above a whisper.

"Then be happy for me."

"Have you considered the risks?" She pulled her hand from his grasp.

"If there's anything I've learned, life is full of risks. We aren't guaranteed the next day or the next breath. But God's taking care of things for us." Jonathan reached for her shoulders, but she stepped back.

"Until the rug gets yanked out from under us on His whim." Her voice quavered.

"Liv, God's not like that."

"So you want to put yourself in danger again?"

"I'm not doing anything stupid. I know what I'm doing." How else could he make her understand?

LYNETTE SOWELL

is an award-winning author with New England roots, but she makes her home in central Texas with her husband and a herd of five cats. When she's not writing, she edits medical reports and chases down stories for the local newspaper. You can find out more about Lynette at lynettesowell.com, or find her on Facebook.

LYNETTE SOWELL

Love's Stormy Gale

HEARTSONG
PRESENTS

Recycling programs
for this product may
not exist in your area.

 ™ LOVE INSPIRED BOOKS

ISBN-13: 978-0-373-48659-5

LOVE'S STORMY GALE

www.LoveInspiredBooks.com

Printed in U.S.A.

There is no fear in love. But perfect love drives out fear, because fear has to do with punishment. The one who fears is not made perfect in love.
—*1 John* 4:18

For my sisters Catherine and Amy, in honor of
one "Perfect Storm" of a whale watch.

Prologue

"Two more weeks, and I'll be Mrs. Robby O'Leary." Olivia Shea twirled on the dais before the full-length mirror in the dress shop, loving the sheen of her satin wedding gown. It was the stuff of dreams, the embodiment of her own dream ever since she'd been a little girl. The ball-gown skirt billowed from her waist to a long train. She stopped the twirl and posed for her maid of honor. "So, Mag, what do you think?"

Maggie Donovan nodded, her smile stretching across her face. Mag had started her own fairytale life with her hero last year. "He'll step right off the boat and sweep you up in his arms and carry you off."

"Smelling of fish and three days without a shower? I don't think so." Olivia snorted at the idea but grinned anyway. "No sweeping until after he cleans up."

At that, Maggie laughed and glanced down at her buzzing phone. "I need to take this. Then I get to cram into my gown."

"Oh, stop. You're gorgeous." Olivia waved Maggie off as her friend stepped closer to the main door of the bridal shop.

Olivia glanced past Maggie out the front window and took in the sight of the cobbled streets of downtown Fairport. Despite the weather, her heart warmed as the rain pounded the stones and the street and drummed on the buildings. Wind lashed at the branches of the elms surrounding Fairport Square. But the sun might as well have been out, shining down in its June summer glory.

No mere thunderstorm could have kept Olivia from one last fitting. Next week she'd meet the photographer for the formal portraits according to the schedule in her phone. Then the Saturday after that... No more stealing just one more kiss at the door when Robby dropped her off at her apartment after supper with his parents. Olivia felt a blush flow across her face. She ached for the security of Robby's arms, even now. How long until his boat returned? If the weather wasn't so bad today, she'd head over to the harbor and wait until she saw the *Lady Jane* chug home to port.

But she had too much to do before the wedding to spend time scanning a stormy horizon. Besides the wedding, they had to close on their house. Two bedrooms and a sun porch, with a yard big enough to need a riding lawn mower.

They'd weather this storm like any other. A nice payday would make their week of separation worth it.

The front door opened, filling the room with the sound of rain on pavement and a shot of humidity. Frances O'Leary, bundled in a raincoat and hat, burst into the tranquil store. Her umbrella was a twisted mass of nylon and metal. She cast it onto the floor.

"Frances, what's wrong?" Olivia's future mother-in-law had never attended one of Olivia's dress fittings, and Olivia couldn't imagine why the woman had ventured out today.

This afternoon Frances's wrinkles looked as though someone had engraved her facial lines more deeply with a chisel. "Liv, something's happened."

Olivia's heart broke out into an uneven gallop. She clutched at her chest. Seed pearls tickled her fingertips. The lacework alone had cost hundreds. Her fingers touched the beads, the sequins. "Did you hear from Robby?" She sounded like a stammering schoolgirl.

"It's the *Lady Jane*." Frances sank onto a nearby pink upholstered chair, oblivious to the rainwater puddling around her. "Didn't you hear?"

"No, what's going on?" Olivia moved her hands to her skirt. Despite herself, she gripped the soft fabric. She glanced at Maggie, heading back to where she stood on the dais.

"Oh, Liv." Maggie gave a sob, then clamped her hand over her mouth. "That was Todd on the phone."

"The distress signal was triggered early this morning. The *Lady Jane's* been lost." Frances spoke the words to the carpet in front of her.

Lost.

The word echoed into Olivia's soul. Did that mean the men had no directions to guide them home? Lost could mean anything, as in, they could be found. Maybe once the weather cleared, they'd chart a course home. GPS could help locate anyone, anywhere.

"But the men?"

"The Coast Guard picked up only one survivor," said Frances.

"Robby?" *Breathe. Try to breathe.*

Frances bowed her head. The woman's unspoken answer ripped a scream from Olivia's lips. She'd never heard a sound like that before. She sank down onto the billowing skirt. It would wrinkle, but it didn't matter. Nothing did.

In the circle of Maggie's arms, Liv buried her face on her friend's shoulder and screamed again. "No, no, no!"

Chapter 1

Two years later

Olivia grasped the ship's railing until her knuckles turned white. She filled her lungs with the salty air, then slowly released her breath. A balmy June breeze whistled in her ears. *Calm down. Now.* She faced the ship's bow as they traveled east, away from Fairport Harbor. Sun sparkled off the rippling water.

A familiar longboat chugged past them. Dad! Olivia released one hand long enough to wave at her father, heading out to check his lobster pots. Then she clamped her hand back around the railing. There went the ice company, more docks, more fishing boats, their trawling nets wrapped up as their captains brought in the catch.

For you, Dad. I came for you. Olivia battled the old ache, as she had every day since returning to Fairport. With the close of the school year in Pennsylvania, she'd bid her middle school biology students good-bye, loaded up her car and headed back to Massachusetts. Perhaps if she closed her eyes, she could imagine the waves turning into the green rolling hills near Harrisburg. Waves of grassy hills couldn't swallow someone you love and tear them from you forever.

She shivered at the idea of being out on the ocean again. Olivia willed herself to relax her hold on the railing. *Lord, help me make it through this trip. The glory of Your creation is around me, but part of me wants to jump in my car and head back to Pennsylvania.*

Above the rushing water and clicking cameras and chattering tourists came Maggie's unmistakable voice over the loudspeaker.

"Today our vessel is piloted by Captain Jonathan Barrotta. Say hello, Jonathan!" The deafening ship's horn was his reply.

Olivia deserved stony silence from her old friends. She wasn't surprised that so far neither of them had acknowledged her presence on the boat. Their boss Terry must have mentioned that she would be on board today, a trial run to see how she coped on the water. She'd been honest with Terry when he hired her, that the idea of being on the water was terrifying. But she was the expert on whales he needed, even without an advanced degree.

She entered the large enclosed cabin that hosted a few café tables facing the windows outside and a small snack bar. Even inside, Olivia could hear Maggie's voice pointing out harbor seals and other wildlife. *Face it, girl. You're not irreplaceable.* Life had gone on. Olivia sighed, and ordered ginger ale and crackers from the snack bar. She found an empty table and slid onto a vacant seat.

Life had also gone on without Robby, as she had known it would. Being back in Fairport, and out on the water, made memories of him come rushing back with the force of a tsunami. Time had dulled the edge of pain, but its assault was overwhelming nonetheless.

Maggie breezed into the snack bar area and headed for the

coffeepot. Olivia turned to face the window. Maybe Maggie hadn't spotted her.

"Liv! It *is* you!" She was engulfed in a hug, and a paper cup filled with coffee appeared next to the ginger ale.

"Maggie." Olivia swallowed hard. Her best friend, a comfort and source of humor during Olivia's grief. She'd missed Maggie these past couple of years.

"I thought it was you I saw in the crowd earlier. You getting your sea legs back?" Maggie's brown eyes sparkled.

"I'm doing well, considering it's the first time I've been out on the water in ages. Dad says it's like riding a bike, though I can't say I've ever seen him ride one." She shook her head at the mental image of her weather-beaten father clad in rubber hip boots and riding a bicycle to the docks every day.

"How is your dad? I haven't seen him around town lately. But since Todd and I started working on the house, we haven't had time for much else." Maggie took the seat across from Olivia.

"So you're working on renovations. That's good to hear. I know you were talking about it before I left." The boat smacked against a wave and her stomach lurched. Olivia leaned on the table to steady herself. She'd forgotten how even a ninety-foot cruise boat could get tossed by the waves.

"Mmm-hmm! Even Jonathan pitches in when he has a moment." Then Maggie rubbed her stomach. "Plus, come December, there'll be three Donovans in the house."

Olivia felt a smile stretch across her face. "Wow, that's wonderful."

Rosy-cheeked Maggie nodded. "I'm glad you're back. Really. And not just for when I go on maternity leave."

Olivia shifted her gaze to the package of saltines. "I don't know how long I'll be working for Whale Tales. I told Terry I'd stay until the end of the summer at least, until the tourist rush slows down. And then I start my graduate program again."

Maggie tugged on Olivia's arm. "Hey, speaking of Jonathan, you should come up to the wheelhouse and see him. He'll be glad to see you."

Olivia looked at the stairs leading to the wheelhouse and resisted. "Maybe some other time. I've got all summer." She smiled, trying to be casual. One memory at a time, thank you very much.

"Well, I figured because he was practically one of your best friends besides me, you'd want to see him."

"It's just—" Olivia broke off mid-sentence. She could readily conjure up an image of Jonathan—curly ebony hair, snappy dark chocolate eyes that crinkled at the corners when he grinned. He smiled the most when piloting, and Olivia imagined he didn't look much different from his Portuguese ancestors at the helm of a boat. She could picture his scruff of beard because he'd run late some mornings and hadn't had time to shave. He probably still wore flannel shirts, sleeves rolled up to the elbows, over ancient T-shirts and equally ancient blue jeans.

Maggie interrupted Olivia's pondering. "You can run, but you can't hide." Her friend's mouth sealed into a firm line.

"Right, Maggie. Now, don't you have some travelers to entertain? We should see some minke whales soon. Or aren't they feeding this close to shore right now?"

"Fine." Maggie frowned, then stood and smoothed the hem of her Whale Tales polo shirt. "And you're right about the whales. We're nearly there. See you after the trip?"

Olivia nodded and watched Maggie climb the stairs to the wheelhouse. Seems all she'd done these past two years was run away. Making amends wouldn't be easy. *Lord knows my mouth hasn't changed any.* And knowing Jonathan, he wouldn't waste words. He would only look at her with an irritated or angry expression, depending on how she goaded him.

Quite different from Robby, who used to enjoy friendly verbal sparring, just so they could make up. At eighteen, she'd fallen in love with Robby the first time she'd seen him from the window of the Seaside Gift Shop. He'd caught her staring as he piloted his father's boat into the harbor. Olivia swallowed her humiliation and introduced herself to him on the dock. Still smelling of the sea and its wildness, he'd charmed her with his wide smile and friendly demeanor.

Six summers later with her undergraduate biology studies behind her, Olivia would have changed her name to Mrs. Robert O'Leary. Two years after the loss of the *Lady Jane* had been long enough to assuage the pain into a dull ache that would only spring up on gray days.

"What have I gotten myself into?" She should have taken the motion sickness medicine. Waves of memory jumbled her insides more than the ocean waves. Despite memories, she'd work this job and make the best of reassembling her life in Fairport. Dad needed her, and she wouldn't be yet another woman to walk out of his life.

The deck pitched under her feet as she went out into the fresh air. A cry went out, "Whales at ten o'clock just off the port bow!"

"Liv's down there, Jon."

Maggie didn't have to tell him. Jonathan could see her silken ponytail bobbing up and down as she talked to a young child, pointing off the bow at the feeding humpback whale. No wonder she'd become a teacher. He caught her radiant grin as she faced the excited child. Jonathan felt himself smile, too, then he sobered. Olivia and Robby should have had a house full of little ones. Jonathan should have been the one…

He banished any more should-haves from his mind and concentrated on the boat.

Jonathan maneuvered closer to the whales so the passengers had a better view. They had paid good money to see the animals in their natural habitat, so he'd make sure they got their show. He never tired of seeing the flukes emerge from the depths of the Atlantic, or the sight of a humpback's tail pointing straight up into the sky.

Maggie continued her narration of the whales' activities,

and the crowd gasped in delight as Spoon, one of the larger humpbacks, showed off her tail with its proud white flukes. Was it Jonathan's imagination, or did he see Olivia turn her face up toward where he stood?

"Quite a show today, huh?" Maggie muted the loudspeaker. "Terry signed Olivia on to work for the summer."

"Really?" Terry had been evasive about their newest naturalist. The Cetacean Institute of Cape Ann had been short-handed with volunteers that summer, but Terry had assured him a CICA associate would be on board each *Whale Tales* voyage to narrate and answer questions about whale facts. "I didn't know. She's a smart lady. Knows a lot about fish."

"Mammals, Jonathan. Whales are not fish. They're mammals."

"Okay, Mag. They're mammals. They bear live young, have scant hair growth, produce milk." Jonathan gladly traded banter with Maggie instead of discussing their old friend Olivia.

"You're forgiven. Come for supper tonight? Todd's barbecuing."

"Sure. Haven't gotten around to writing my grocery list anyway." The ship's radio squawked—more humpbacks farther south.

Maggie notified the passengers of the sighting, and without being asked, Jonathan turned south and pushed on the throttle. He was sure Maggie hadn't finished her comments about Olivia.

"You know something, Jon?"

"Hmm?"

"I wasn't sure what to think when I saw Olivia again. But Terry seems to think she can handle it."

"What's that?"

"Being out on the water. You probably won't be her pilot all the time."

"Won't be a problem for me. I can handle it." Like he'd confess to Maggie that he'd missed Olivia so bad he could feel the pain to his very heart. They'd all lost Robby, felt it in different ways.

Maggie grinned as she picked up the microphone. "Good. I know you'll look out for her."

He grunted a response. He glanced down at the railing where Olivia stood. She'd taken the hat off and let her hair down.

Only Olivia's knowledge of cetaceans rivaled Maggie's. Too bad Olivia had withdrawn her application for the dual master's and doctorate program and moved away. Too bad about a lot of things.

Twenty minutes had passed since the course change. Another whale-watching vessel appeared like a toy ship in the distance, but Olivia could see the whales breaching, their massive bodies arching out of the water and smashing back into the sea. White spray shot into the sky with the impact of the hulking gray bodies.

The beauty of the whales brought a lump to her throat. If they weren't worshiping their Creator, Olivia didn't know what to call it. Again and again the humpbacks performed their boisterous celebration. *Lord, I see Your majesty out here. These animals are so wildly beautiful, by Your design. You care for them. You care for me. Help me to remember that when I'm afraid.* She swallowed at the thought of her pills in the backpack. Just one pill, and she could breathe again. She had seen a doctor in Pennsylvania and had been on medication to help with panic attacks. She hadn't needed them in months. But now might be an appropriate time…

The waves rocked the idling ship, and Olivia's eyes followed their undulating movement. Seventy feet of water below them to the bottom of the ocean. Farther out the water went still deeper, farther out where Robby's body—

Olivia found her way past a family of passengers and into the cabin. With a swig from the bottled water in her pack, she washed down a pill, then sank onto a bench by the wall.

She would not let them see her cry. Instead, she would battle her way through the memories. Until now, she thought she'd been winning. *Big baby.*

Jonathan saw Olivia clumsily disappear into the cabin. She didn't come out for the remainder of the trip. He didn't recall her ever being susceptible to seasickness in the past.

After they returned to port and docked and the passengers had disembarked, Jonathan entered the cabin to find Olivia huddled in a corner booth, her chin resting on her knees, her sunglasses hiding her eyes. Stray hairs had wafted across one cheek. Her even breathing told him she'd fallen asleep.

Olivia started and sat up. She took off her sunglasses and met Jonathan's gaze. "I guess I fell asleep."

"Are you all right?" He focused on Olivia's nose as he touched her shoulder. He would drown in her eyes for sure if he let her hold his gaze.

She sat up straighter, shaking off his touch. "I'm fine. Thanks." She stood up. "Good to see you." She moved past him and left the cabin.

Jonathan watched out the window. Olivia trotted down the dock to the parking lot where an ancient Corolla waited. She peeled out of the parking lot, spraying crushed shells in her wake. He'd waited for her to come back to Fairport. But her emotional walls had grown higher over time. Right now, he had no idea how to break them down—or if he even wanted to try. His own memories were filed away in a forgotten corner of his mind. Renewing a friendship with Olivia would only cause the past to return unrestrained.

Home. Olivia hadn't understood the full meaning of the word until now. The small gray Cape Cod house greeted her like an old weathered friend. Seeing it again caused a warm sensation to fill Olivia to her toes.

An only child raised by a fisherman might have had what some considered a lonely life, but Olivia never thought so.

She recalled staying with Mrs. Flaherty next door if her father sailed late. She grew up loving books and games and didn't mind playing alone.

Her little car ground to a stop at the curb. Olivia rubbed her forehead. Seeing Jonathan had rattled her but good. Her first impulse had been to throw herself into his arms and hug him with two years of missing him. Then she'd pushed him away, confirming everyone's assumptions that Olivia was back, prickly as ever. The memories had ebbed, but being vulnerable to Jonathan made her run.

Cooking supper for Dad would give her a breather. Olivia locked her car, then trudged to the house. She put on some soft music, and minutes later was up to her elbows in homemade pasta dough. A trip to the market that morning had yielded a fresh catch of clams. Olivia put the stockpot on to steam. She was feeling better already, she realized as she fed the dough into the pasta maker.

"How's my girl?" her father's voice called, taking her back uncounted years with his old greeting.

"Great, Pop! I'm making clams Alfredo with linguine." The aroma made her stomach rumble.

Her dad eased a suspender off one shoulder as he entered the kitchen. "Smells good." His brown gaze darted around the kitchen; wrinkles lined his smile. "But it's been a long time since the kitchen looked this messy."

"Don't worry, I'll take care of it all." She grinned, remembering her tendency to let the dishes go.

When supper had finished cooking, Olivia joined her father at the old dining table. As she ate her clams and pasta and tossed salad, Olivia watched her father's hands as he twirled the noodles with his fork.

As much as she hated the thought, she realized her father was growing old. The knuckles of his hands, swollen and callused, spoke of his years of hard work. Yet he didn't complain; only every now and then he rubbed his fingers.

Someday she'd be all alone.

"Why so serious looking all of a sudden?" her dad quizzed.

"I was just thinking." How could she tell her father that she thought of him as an old man?

"Well, don't think so hard. It looks painful." His gruff tone was offset by the twinkle in his eyes.

Trust her dad to joke about what was on her mind. Olivia had to laugh to herself as she scrubbed the pots and pans later on. He would make fun of serious situations. But that didn't work. Olivia had tried, but humor made a poor balm to cover old pain.

After she left the dishes on the rack, and pots and pans drying on towels spread on the counter, Olivia went into the formal parlor. Pictures covered with a thin film of dust still covered the mantel, and one on the end caught her eye. The picture still packed a punch.

The three of them stood on the pier next to her father's boat. She couldn't recall who'd taken the snapshot. Her mother clutched her father's arm and wore a pasted-on smile, the same kind Olivia used when putting on a brave face. Olivia, probably two years of age, was perched on her father's shoulders.

How long after that photograph was taken did her mother leave them? Olivia didn't know, but she remembered seeing a snapshot of her fourth birthday, with just she and her father sitting in front of a birthday cake.

Olivia set her jaw and glared at the picture of the trio that had once been. "I'm not like you, Ma. I came back."

Chapter 2

"Give me a couple o' months, Pete, and I'll have a down payment for the *Isabella Rose*." Jonathan sipped from his coffee cup and set it back on the wooden counter. He'd have to hurry to make it to the dock on time. But a man couldn't beat the breakfast at the Sea Dawg, or the deal he was about to iron out with Pete.

"Good deal, man. The wife's been after me t' open a tackle shop or somethin'. Don't want me out there anymore. At least I'm gettin' out of the business with life and limb, and can fin'ly get a little peace at home." The fisherman rubbed the stubble on his chin and made a huffing sound. "Plus she's tired of going to all the kids' ball games by herself."

"All right, I'll look you up before the end of the summer." Jonathan swallowed the last of his coffee.

The men exchanged nods as Jonathan picked up his breakfast ticket.

The balmy summer air outside reminded him again of the simple gifts of life. Simple, yet priceless. Another morning to give thanks for being alive. Jonathan fended off the memory of his father's phone call the night before. "I want more for you, Jon. Trawling is a fruitless struggle against the sea and the bureaucrats who try to tell a man when and where and how much to fish. I'm glad your mother and I retired to Florida," his father had said.

The exchange of words that followed reminded him of Olivia's sharp tones her first day on a tour the week before. Since then she'd avoided him, and he couldn't blame her. He had assumed they were better friends than for her to ignore him. Jonathan decided to put his assumptions aside.

Instead, he would start counting the days until Pete's boat was his. The open sea beckoned like an old friend. A fickle friend, yes, but Jonathan knew better than to try to tame its wildness. Things happened on the water and sometimes men and women didn't come home from their voyages. That was life. He could deal with it, and he hoped Olivia could, too. In God's hands wherever he went, Jonathan would keep shipping out and fishing. When it was his time to tell planet Earth good-bye, it was time.

At least he and Olivia hadn't been assigned to the same boat so far. He wasn't sure about her emotional ability to handle being out on the ocean again, no matter how Maggie had assured him that Olivia could do it.

Jonathan still remembered Olivia's tenacity to jump in with her whole self, holding nothing back. It drew him to her like a magnet, even now, when too much remained unsaid between them. He quickened his steps to the docks and tried to push Olivia from his mind.

Jonathan's lighthearted whistle coming from inside the boat made Olivia's pulse jump. *Scaredy cat.* There was nothing to fear, from Jonathan or anything else on a sunny summer day like today. She paused at the cabin door to watch customers line up at the dock. Their excitement made the air crackle, and Lord willing, she and Jonathan would find them some whales.

After Jonathan recovered from the shock of realizing she was working his boat of course.

A wry smile tugged at her lips. Olivia fought the urge and headed for the source of the whistling. She entered the cabin.

Jonathan's back faced her; curly dark hair ruffled in the light breeze filtering through the doorway.

He whirled around, and as expected, stopped his whistling. "Liv."

The familiar nickname came out in a hoarse rasp.

Olivia's first impression was how good Jonathan looked, even better than an unbidden memory or the quick glimpse last week on the boat. His face and arms glowed a ruddy bronze from hours on the water. But his dark molasses eyes wore a guarded expression, as if he were encountering a wounded animal. She'd hurt him by leaving, she knew. The other day when they'd first seen each other, she hadn't allowed herself to take in the sight of him, as she was doing now.

Her voice came out in a croak. "Maggie didn't feel well this morning, so I'm covering her tour."

Jonathan gave a noncommittal nod and turned back toward the open engine room door.

Olivia didn't ask if he minded her presence. She could see his broad shoulders tighten and tug at his T-shirt. It wasn't like she'd volunteered to tour with him. If anything, she had steered clear of Jonathan since that first whale watch. Facing the past was hard enough. Seeing Jonathan again and pretending the past hadn't happened was another matter.

"So, how long have you been piloting?"

"A year and a half or so." Jonathan's thick capable fingers snapped his toolbox shut. "Had to do something to make a living. I help with an occasional fishing charter. Nothing major." He used a rag to wipe his greasy fingernails, gave up and tossed it onto the toolbox. He moved past her.

Who was giving whom the cold shoulder now? She pattered after him, feeling much like a puppy trotting after an annoyed older dog. So he'd started piloting for Terry's whale tours six months after she'd left town.

"Look," she called out, "if you don't want me here, just say so. Maybe Terry can find someone else."

"I never said you weren't welcome."

"Okay." Olivia swallowed hard. "This isn't easy for me. Being out here, I mean. But it's something I have to do. I have to be out with the whales again."

Jonathan nodded. She noted his strong jaw clench and unclench. "How's your dad?"

"Good." She mentally snuffed out a wispy flame of concern for her father's health, and pulled the touring notes from her briefcase. Her real reason for coming home, the one thing that goaded her into facing her fears: something was wrong with Dad. No matter, he went out day after day to check his lobster pots. But he'd been coughing and had lost weight.

"Has he been having a pretty good season so far?" Yet another question from Jonathan.

"I don't know. He hasn't said, but then even when times are good, Dad lives like a miser. But he eats out too much. And you wouldn't believe the junk food and frozen dinners in the freezer." Olivia shook her head.

"Sounds like my fridge."

Olivia noticed Jonathan's slight grin. Her throat caught, and she swallowed hard. He'd been lonely, too.

"Maybe I'll cook supper for all of us like I used to." She couldn't believe she'd spoken the words aloud.

"I'd be there, like I used to be."

Olivia refused to think of Robby, the other former member of the "three musketeers" who used to haunt the Shea house at suppertime. "I'll let you know. Sometime." She turned to her notes, reassembling her composure. They couldn't go back. Old times had come and gone.

A grief counselor had told her once about a "new normal" after losing Robby. But just exactly what that normal was, Olivia couldn't fathom.

She was already getting seasick and they hadn't even left the dock. Why else would she feel so queasy and quivery inside? Olivia headed down the narrow metal stairs to the cabin below. As soon as the passengers had boarded, Olivia began what she called her "Whale Story" and introduced the morning's staff. The fore and aft mates stood at their respective places on the ship, and the third busily took orders at the snack bar.

Meanwhile Olivia continued a delicate verbal dance with Jonathan during the first part of the trip, as if they were venturing closer, being friendlier. Then the past would loom up again, and they'd circle away.

Olivia delivered the usual harbor narration as they passed landmarks of Fairport's harbor. She spoke too quickly, she knew, when she pointed out the fisherman statue. The memorial to the town's fishermen who perished over the past centuries caused a stab of remembrance that threatened to interfere with her forced calm.

Now that she'd been out on the water, Olivia enjoyed the sensation of skimming across the waves. She had missed this. From the smiles on the faces she could see below, most of the passengers shared her enjoyment.

Jonathan busied himself with the latest weather forecast, even though he had checked the printout not thirty minutes ago.

The wind whistled through the open windows and tugged at Olivia's hair. Her eyebrows furrowed as she read Maggie's notes. Jonathan wanted to smooth the anxiety from her face and allow his fingers to touch the wayward wisp.

He recalled the last time he'd touched her hair. He had run his fingers through the silken strands. Olivia, in his arms like he'd always dreamed. Except she was saying good-bye, running from the pain of loss that plagued them both. Now that she had returned, what would happen?

The confines of the pilothouse caused them to rub elbows.

Jonathan wondered how he'd survive a summer of seeing Olivia day after day. She could never know the nights he'd lain awake, missing her. He had battled his longing into submission, and until now he'd assumed it was dead.

He liked his life the way it was now. His feelings for Olivia needed to stay in the past.

Jonathan cast a glance in her direction. Pink suffused Olivia's cheeks while he allowed his glance to linger.

Until the boat reached the open water, Olivia kept up such a stream of chatter that Jonathan hoped she didn't pass out from lack of breath. She hit verbal overdrive when describing the fisherman statue. He caught himself grinning.

"What? What is it?" Olivia's gaze bored into him. "You're laughing at me."

"How do you do it?"

"What's that?"

"Keep talking so fast without turning blue."

She snorted. "I don't talk that fast."

"Uh-huh. Next time I'll clock you on it."

"Right. Whatever." She made a face, then looked at the horizon and smiled.

They both saw the minke whale in the distance, a swift, sleek black body with a small dorsal fin disturbing the waves. The passengers pointed and gestured.

After reaching Stellwagen Bank, a nearby section of ocean known for its whale population, they had no difficulty spotting a small group of humpbacks about one hundred yards off the starboard bow. As Olivia continued her narration, Jonathan forced himself to focus on the workings of the ship. Other whale-watching tours were still en route to Stellwagen and radioed him. He advised them of the whales' location.

The clang of feet scaling the metal stairway to the wheelhouse caught Jonathan's attention. Brad, one of the summer interns who helped with the snack bar, stuck his head in the door. "Capt'n, the engine's sounding kind of funny."

"I'll check it out. Take the helm, Liv."

Fear flickered across her face for an instant. She muted the microphone. "All right."

Jonathan followed Brad down to the main deck where he saw a few faces filled with concern. Most of the passengers, though, were focusing on the whale activity. The engine chugged and spluttered.

Olivia's voice continued over the sound system, although Jonathan heard a hint of hesitation in her speech. Good. At least she'd kept up with the program. He unlocked the door to the engine room. The pungent smell of diesel fuel nearly bowled him over as the engine gave a final cough, then died. Flooded engine. He found the toolbox and started working. After twenty minutes of tinkering, Jonathan realized he needed to contact another boat to be nearby for safety's sake at least.

"Brad, get Tim and Caitlin and meet me in the wheelhouse," Jonathan said to the young man hovering nearby.

Now to break the news to Olivia. He breathed a quick prayer as he crossed the deck to the stairs. Jonathan headed up to the wheelhouse, pushing through the door. Olivia's face had paled. One trembling hand held the wheel, the other her microphone.

Olivia's knees had turned to jelly. She hated it when that happened.

Jonathan touched her arm. "Hey, you okay?"

She nodded. The rhythm of the waves rocked the boat side to side, back to front, side to side. "I'm fine now. Don't worry about me. How's the engine?"

"Flooded. But no worries, we'll get it restarted in a few moments."

After Jonathan restarted the boat, the rest of the voyage seemed to take twice as long. She kept Jonathan at bay by sticking to her script, and making notations of the whales she'd seen. One of the females had a new calf. New to her anyway. Jonathan might know the name of the youngster, but Olivia decided to wait until they returned to shore and ask Terry about the humpback.

Too much had happened, Olivia guessed, to repair even a semblance of the friendship she and Jonathan used to have. Robby had been an integral part of their relationship. With him gone, they didn't have anything left in common.

Relief swept over her when they docked in the harbor.

She wouldn't let herself think what she had years ago. *Why hadn't Jonathan been the one lost at sea instead of Robby?* She didn't want to lose him either.

When she pulled her car to a stop at the house, she saw her dad's pickup truck in the driveway.

"Pop, I'm home." She could hear his snore filtering back from the front room. She heard a grunt, then a rustling noise— he'd probably fallen asleep reading the paper. Olivia opened the refrigerator door to unload some groceries she'd picked up on the way home.

Her father entered the kitchen. "Had a good catch today. Kept back a couple of two-pounders for supper, if you want to steam 'em later."

"Sounds good. Did you get a good price at the market?"

"Good enough." His lined face wrinkled into a smile. "You had a bit of trouble today?"

Olivia had never learned to play poker. Besides detesting gambling, she couldn't mask her feelings very well. "We broke down about fifteen miles out. Jonathan got the engine started again."

"Ah, so you did end up on one of his boats."

"What's that supposed to mean?" She gingerly reached around the lobster for a can of soda. Good thing its pincers were secured with a rubber band.

"I think it's a good idea if you and he work on a boat to- gether." With creaking joints, her father settled onto one of the kitchen chairs.

"Is that so? What if I don't think so?" Olivia washed the soda can lid, then popped it open.

"You lost your nerve." His wise old eyes filled with concern. "And being with that Barrotta boy will help you get it back again." Olivia turned to the window over the sink. She could barely make out the harbor's edge beyond a small stand of trees.

"I don't know, Dad. It's not that simple." She didn't want to upset him by dredging up more of the past.

"You've got the ocean in your blood, Liv. No matter how far you run, you won't be rid of it." Her father stood and crossed the tiny kitchen. He chucked Olivia under her chin. "Okay, kid? You got the guts to handle this. I know it."

She nodded absently and began to prepare supper. Did Jonathan have to muster up the nerve to pilot the sea? Or had he already conquered the gnawing fear?

Chapter 3

Cold, dark water swallowed them like a ravenous beast. The boat had rolled end over end, weighed down by the catch. Shouts. Tumbling equipment. Shattering glass as the wheelhouse flooded. Sky and water blended as one.

He had to get out. Jonathan gulped a deep breath before the room flooded. His boots weighed him down like bricks. His jacket hampered his arms like a straitjacket. He sensed rather than saw Robby flailing for freedom from their water-filled prison. Please God, let the distress beacon start working. Jonathan wiggled through a broken window. Searing pain ground down the length of his leg. He disregarded the cut; the water's chill numbed the pain, but his brain fought the instinct to surrender to the darkness. Where was the surface? He blew a few precious bubbles, feeling them head upward. That way. Jonathan kicked harder.

Lungs burning, arms on fire, he broke surface. God, please don't let a roller take me under. How long until help came? The storm raged on, and Jonathan begged that his friends would

*soon surface. Then came another wave. He didn't know if he
could hold on. God, help me. Where was Robby? Where were
the others? He could see the angry water coming at him—*

Moonlight streamed into his open bedroom window.

Jonathan kicked the sweat-soaked sheet off his body, then
filled his lungs with air as he swung his legs over the side
of the bed. A long scar on his right leg from the knee to the
top of the thigh remained, a reminder of the night he'd nearly
lost his life.

The ocean outside glistened, its surface spangled with di-
amonds of light from the full moon. The normally soothing
view at the bottom of the hill didn't help when he had nightmares. "God, I don't know why I'm here. Two years now, and
I haven't done anything worth living for. Piloting a tour boat.
I want my own boat, Lord. I want to be on the ocean. But I
can't do it alone. I can't do it without Your help." Jonathan
raked his hand through his hair, and rubbed the stubble on
his chin. He wouldn't have had this dream again had Olivia
not come home. Did she still have nightmares, or could she
finally sleep?

To share a life with him, a woman would have to understand the life of a fisherman. Long hours without contact,
fluctuating pay, no guarantee of the future. Not to mention
the occupational hazards; commercial fishing had a high mor-
tality rate compared to other jobs.

But when the fish came, all thoughts of the risks vanished.
Jonathan couldn't wait until he owned Pete Celucci's boat.
He'd save his earnings, find another boat and sell the first one
eventually—then start building his own dream house. Even
if he had to do it alone.

Olivia woke with a pounding headache. The scare with
the boat's engine yesterday reminded her why. Her selfish-
ness scalded her conscience. Jonathan had lost his best friend,
and had stayed in the place where he'd have to face constant
reminders of all he'd lost. Olivia had played chicken and run

away. Anger at her own cowardice caused her head to throb even more.

She rolled over and looked at her clock, bolted upright, then clutched her forehead. Another tension headache hit her, and she was late for work.

Terry was sporting a glare when she entered the office. His mustache fairly bristled. "We've delayed the morning trip for you."

"Sorry." Her head pounded.

"You look horrible."

"I'll be okay."

"Go ahead, get out there."

Jonathan was performing the final checks on the boat as the passengers milled at the dock. "About time," someone murmured as Olivia passed. Would today be better than yesterday? It would have to be.

Jonathan had retreated into his own shell, it seemed. Olivia noticed the dark circles under his eyes. He hadn't slept well, and a quick pang jabbed at her conscience. Had it been her fault? She wouldn't ask. He kept his dark brown eyes focused on the horizon, then on the whales, but never at her for more than a split second.

No problem. It seemed they'd done more spatting with each other than anything since renewing their friendship. She needed to find more friends and move on with her life. She went to her church on Sunday mornings, although she had yet to attend any of the singles group activities. It wasn't the same. People had paired off, gotten married and moved on. But there was Maggie and Todd's upcoming Fourth of July party. She'd go to that. Even if Jonathan showed, Olivia could find other people to spend time with. She needed that new normal.

The morning dragged on. Over half the boat got sick, and Olivia's stomach heaved once they were out about a dozen miles.

* * *

That night after supper, Olivia sat on the front porch swing with her father, talking about the day and drinking iced tea. Olivia drank the tea, and her father told her stories of the market.

"Still was a shame, what happened to Rob O'Leary Senior. He would rather have gone down with his boat than lose his mind a little at a time." Her dad puffed on his pipe, an old habit not yet relinquished despite Olivia's expressed concern. She bit her lip as the smoke curled around their heads. Soon the pungent aroma would drive her inside.

"I wish you'd told me." Olivia sighed. "Poor Frances, all alone. She must blame me even more."

Dad puffed another small cloud of smoke, then returned the sigh. "Didn't want to bring it up. I didn't know if you were ever moving back home." He punctuated the statement with a cough.

"I see." Why had it taken her this long? Olivia bit her lip before she replied. "Robby and I weren't trying to hurt her feelings by wanting our own home."

"Course not. You wanted your own nest. Better that way anyhow. Rob used to complain about Frances's heavy-handed ways 'til we begged him to stow it."

"Oh." She'd been right, then, when she told Robby years ago that his mom would run their lives if they moved in with her. Robby agreed, though reluctantly, she recalled. If they married and lived with his parents until Olivia finished her education, Frances would be cooking and cleaning for them all. Probably even laying out Robby's fishing clothes for him, and trotting behind Olivia to point out her multiple shortcomings.

"Anyhow...what's done is done." Her father puffed.

Olivia planted a kiss on her father's forehead. "I'll get started on the dishes."

He grinned, clenching the pipe between his teeth. "Smoke getting to you?"

She nodded as she went inside, the screen door smacking

closed behind her. No use arguing or pleading with him. She'd even shown her dad articles about the dangers of pipe smoke, but he had only waved them off. Olivia gave up.

The dishwasher hummed at last. Olivia could hear the evening news report above the noise of the machine. Dad would fall asleep again, his half-read newspaper spread on his chest, his reading glasses still on his nose.

She passed through the living room on her way up the stairs. Sure enough, Dad had reclined fully in the ancient recliner, his face pointing up at the ceiling, mouth open in a snore. If he didn't wake himself up and turn in on his own later, she'd make sure the TV was turned off and all secured for the night.

The fourth step creaked on the flight of stairs as it always had. Olivia realized she'd enjoyed the familiar sounds of the old house since she'd been home. A sensation of nostalgia wrapped itself around her. Dad sawed his logs downstairs, and she was heading up to do her homework.

She entered her bedroom and awoke her hibernating laptop. No doubt her email had piled up. She couldn't remember if she'd checked it since she'd been home. Only a few personal emails greeted her when she opened the in-box. The rest disappeared with a few clicks of the mouse.

Olivia typed in the web address for the Cetacean Institute of Cape Ann. The institute had a slick website. If she signed on permanently with the group, she would have a chance at a paying research position. Plus, they'd help with graduate school tuition reimbursement, possibly as soon as this fall.

She glanced at the graduate school application on the desk. If she reapplied, her postgraduate credits would still be good, even with interrupting her studies to move away to teach. Within three years, she could be Dr. Olivia Shea, if she worked hard enough. Fear wouldn't keep her from finishing what she'd started.

What would Jonathan think of her dream? Did he have any aspirations of his own? She knew the rumor that he was a jinx, the sole survivor of an ill-fated voyage. Would he try to fish again? An icy prickle skittered down her spine at the thought.

Olivia squeezed her car into the last available spot on the grassy shoulder across the road from Maggie and Todd Donovan's house, which was nestled in a secluded cove. The Atlantic shimmered in the distance. According to Maggie, there was a small beach a short walk from the house. Her parents had given them the property as a wedding gift. Nice parents.

She spotted Jonathan's weathered Jeep in the driveway. Only then did she realize she would be spending the whole day with him, without their work as a distraction. Olivia inhaled slowly, leaning against the headrest. She reminded herself of her resolve to put the past behind. Plus, judging from the dozen or so vehicles clustered on the property, she shouldn't have trouble mixing with the old crowd from church and making some new connections.

Armed with a bowl of potato salad as her contribution to the party, Olivia locked her car and headed up the sidewalk.

"C'mon in!" Todd held the front door open. "Maggie's on the patio setting out the food. Hope you brought your appetite!"

"Sure did."

An explosion of laughter caused Olivia to stand on tiptoe and glance over Todd's shoulder.

"Water balloons," he explained. "One of the college kids brought them."

Olivia followed Todd through the spacious foyer to the large kitchen and entertaining area. One wall with floor-to-ceiling glass windows faced the ocean. Outside on the patio, guests clustered around a long table. Olivia hesitated before joining the group. Todd had already grabbed the tongs for the grill, while she hung back and watched.

Why did she feel like it was the first day of school? She knew most of these people. Yet she hadn't kept in touch with any of them, except for Maggie.

Jonathan's curly hair caught her eye. She saw him laugh, his smile lending warmth to the day. Then he met her eyes through the window. Was it her imagination, or did the grin slightly fade?

The potato salad. Olivia goaded herself out onto the patio and to the food table. She nudged aside a bowl of macaroni salad to make room for her bowl. After accepting a cold soda from Todd, she went inside. If Jonathan wanted to talk to her, he knew she was around.

She immediately chided herself for her attitude. "Don't be ugly, Liv," she mumbled under her breath. "You *will* talk to him when you go outside again. Be civil."

"Talking to yourself again?" Maggie grinned as she sprinkled seasoning on the hamburgers.

"I've been told it's a sign of genius."

"Who are you getting up the nerve to talk to? I could introduce you to this guy I know…"

Olivia groaned and shook her head. "No setups here. Don't do me any favors." The last thing she'd ever try would be going on a blind date.

"Really. He's a nice guy, ambitious, loves the Lord and he's got that George Clooney look going on. As in a young George Clooney."

Olivia grinned at the description. "So where is Mr. Perfect, then?"

"He's the one wearing the Patriots T-shirt."

"Where?"

"Follow me, oh, shortsighted one." Maggie picked up the tray of burgers and headed back to the patio.

They met Todd at the grill. Liv glanced at a group of men talking, then saw the football team logo on Jonathan's shirt. Surely he wasn't the only man in a Pats' shirt?

"Ha. Very funny, Maggie." Olivia's face flamed.

"Oh, but I'm quite serious. Am I right, Todd?" Maggie rubbed Todd's arm.

"Quite right, babe." He hooked an arm around Maggie's waist and gave her a peck on the lips.

Olivia snorted. "That's just great. It's a conspiracy. Jonathan and I have too much history to be a couple."

"But you both understand each other so well." Maggie sounded hopeful. "I think you should give each other some time and a chance."

Olivia grabbed a paper plate and smiled. "I'm going to get a quick bite." She stuffed aside the notion of anything beyond friendship with Jonathan.

Jonathan half listened to a friend talking about his latest trip to Fenway Park for a Red Sox game. Box seats, from his boss, lucky guy. But Olivia had been on Jonathan's mind from the moment he'd seen her arrive, hugging a bowl of what he hoped was potato salad.

But she hadn't greeted him, even though they'd made eye contact right away. He saw Kristi Chamberlain chat with Olivia, then show off her engagement ring. That was one woman he was glad to see get engaged. Evidently she'd gotten over his refusals when she'd asked him out "just for coffee, Jon." When he dated, he wanted to be the one to do the asking. Call him traditional or old-fashioned, but that was the way he liked to date. Now it bordered on ridiculous, between people following each other around online via Facebook, Twitter and such. Whatever happened to a real conversation?

Now Olivia stood with hands on hips, an attractive flush coloring her pretty face. Maggie and Todd were laughing. Jonathan wondered what they'd said to cause such a reaction. Olivia muttered something, then moved back to the food table and grabbed a plate.

Some of the guys were heading down to check out the volleyball game, but just then, Jonathan craved potato salad. Time to check out exactly what was in the bowl that Olivia had brought.

A smile replaced the scowl on Olivia's face as he approached the food table. "Hi." She tapped the edge of a plastic bowl. "I made potato salad."

His mouth watered. "I hoped you did." Jonathan heaped two spoonfuls of potato salad on a fresh paper plate. "I'm going to see if those ribs on the grill are done. Care to join me?"

"Sure."

So far so good. Light conversation and banter flowed around them, but Jonathan noticed Olivia darting quick glances at the other guests. She hadn't approached any of the others, while Jonathan greeted several friends on their trip to the grill. The water balloon enthusiasts were busy drying off.

A puff of smoke greeted them as Todd lifted the cover from the grill. "If you want any meat, come and get it now. After this, fend for yourself."

"And we're first in line." Jonathan held out his plate. "Just don't mess with Liv's potato salad here. I've got first dibs on that." Todd heaped several sauce-covered ribs onto Jonathan's plate.

"Why, thank you." Olivia grinned, eyes sparkling. "I've never had anyone defend my potato salad before." And then she gave a soft chuckle. Her honey-brown hair drifted around her shoulders.

Jonathan felt a stirring within him when she looked into his eyes. He wanted to protect her, shelter her even though he'd been joking. The glimmer in her eye hadn't been there since she'd given such a look to another man, namely Robby. Jonathan shifted his focus to his plate.

Olivia made room for the ribs. "I suppose we could find somewhere to sit?"

"Of course." Jonathan led her to a bench at the edge of the patio. He could see the water from where they sat. A wayward gull flew in their direction, probably hoping for a tidbit of food.

They ate in companionable silence.

"I'm glad you came." Olivia's voice broke the quiet. "I didn't realize until now how I'd lost touch with people here. I've missed out on a lot. Maggie's going to have a baby, Kristi's engaged."

Jonathan swallowed the last bite of barbecued ribs. "Believe it or not, we missed you. I know I did."

Olivia turned to him, her liquid eyes inscrutable in the July sunshine. She laid a hand on his arm, and paused as if she were about to speak.

Maggie stood at the edge of the patio and bellowed, "Okay, everyone! It's time for the scavenger hunt!"

Great. Just when he was ready to kick back. He'd overstuffed himself and wanted to relax a little. Maybe Maggie wouldn't harass them to participate.

But instead Olivia turned to him. "I'm game if you are."

If she'd suggested they try to swim across Massachusetts Bay all the way to Cape Cod, he probably would have taken her up on it. Jonathan found himself tossing his dirty plate in the trash can and looking at a list, while Olivia stood next to him. A tiny crease appeared between her eyes and then disappeared as she smiled at him.

Okay. He'd forgo zoning out for the afternoon. The Red Sox weren't playing this weekend anyway.

Chapter 4

"She wants us to find *what?*" Olivia tried to eye the note in Jonathan's hand and still keep watch on the road that led to town.

"Two tomatoes. We have to go to Market Basket and buy two tomatoes, and we'll get our next instructions." Jonathan tossed the paper between them and cracked his knuckles.

She couldn't believe she'd dragged him along on the indignity of one of Maggie's scavenger hunts. On the other hand, looking for assorted oddities throughout Fairport gave them something to talk about besides the past. Their growing collection from the scavenger hunt included a red-and-white fishing lure, a red T-shirt they'd found at a thrift store, plus a spool of red thread.

"I'm sorry I got you into this."

"Don't apologize." His tentative grin made her focus her attention firmly on the road. She braked behind a carload of teens probably heading to Good Harbor Beach. "I'm in this to win. How about you?"

"Yes, me, too. And I'm having fun getting more involved in the old church group."

Jonathan cleared his throat. "It's changed some. Some have gotten engaged, moved away, dropped out. There's a few of us still hanging around, too old for the college crowd."

"But when the Young Marrieds group gets together, we don't fit with them either."

"No, not exactly." Jonathan's tone made her glance his way. Olivia glimpsed regret in his eyes.

"What is it? Was there someone?" Instead of thinking, she'd spoken aloud. As if she had any right to ask. A warm flush washed through her and she sucked in a deep breath. Back went her gaze to the road.

Jonathan shook his head. "Naw, she and I never got together."

A pang nipped at Olivia's heart. "I'm sorry."

"It's okay. It happens."

She wanted to tell him he deserved someone special, but held her tongue and instead concentrated on finding a vacant parking space in the Market Basket parking lot.

"There's one!" Jonathan jabbed at a spot at the end of a row. "And there's Kevin and Julie running for their car."

Olivia responded by zipping into the parking spot. She shoved thoughts of lost love to the side for the moment. "Let's go."

When they jogged to the store's entrance, Jonathan gripped one of her hands in his rough one, his strength pulling her along.

She pulled up short at the produce aisle, her heart pounding although the dash to the store had been a short one. Her fingers still remembered the texture of Jonathan's hand. Olivia reached for a smooth tomato in the bin.

"Do you see a note anywhere, or do you think someone already got the last clue?" Olivia whirled to see what Jonathan was up to and nearly collided with a sour-faced woman with graying hair. "Oh, Mrs. O'Leary."

"I heard you were back." Frances O'Leary's accusing glare seared Olivia's face more than the summer sun could. Her look passed from Olivia to Jonathan, then back to Olivia again. "Watch her, Jon. She'll push you, too."

Olivia fumbled for the words. She'd had no idea Robby's mother still harbored anger toward her. "I don't know what you mean by push—"

"You pushed Robby into going on that last voyage. Always had to be telling him how to run things, you did. I just wish he'd called off the wedding and forgotten the whole idea."

"I really don't think this is the place to be discussing what happened…" Olivia sensed Jonathan moving closer to her. "I think we should make a fresh start. I'm willing if—"

Frances yanked a plastic produce bag from a nearby roll. "Fresh start. That's easy to say. You're not alone. First I lose Robby, then his father." Frances wore the snarl of a wounded animal.

"Don't talk to Olivia that way. She lost Robby, too. Anyway, Robby wanted to go." Jonathan's words and his warm hand squeezing her shoulder helped take the sting from Frances's words. "And you're not alone. There are lots of people who care about you, too."

Frances slung a bag of unsuspecting tomatoes into the metal shopping cart. "Well, I can see she's already made short work of charming you, too. Watch her, Jon, she's bad news." Shoulders tight, she stomped away, her shoes clicking a staccato beat on the linoleum.

Olivia tried to relax her grip on the two tomatoes. "I never knew she was so angry."

"You can't do anything about her anger. I tried going around to visit her after you left, but when Robby Senior got sicker, Frances started lashing out more and more." He removed his hand from her shoulder. "I'm sorry you had to hear that."

"It would have come out eventually, but thanks for sticking up for me." She reached for a square of paper taped to the lower edge of the tomato bin. "Find Blue Moon at The Music House."

Jonathan grinned. "We've got this game."

She nodded absently, still reeling from the effect of Frances O'Leary's venom. Her first impulse had been a retort to Frances along the lines of, "Talk about pushy, lady, you wrote the book on it." But instead she'd stammered and clung desperately to a remnant of Christian behavior.

"Hey, are you going to be all right? We can stop hunting for stuff and just go back to Maggie's."

Olivia would show him she wouldn't crumble. "No, I want to keep going. I'm fine. Really." She gave him her best smile in reassurance.

A faint pinkish smudge at the western horizon was the only remainder of daylight. Olivia turned to face east, watching the gunmetal gray surf pound the shore. The night sky met the water in a nearly indistinguishable line. A few stars had made an appearance. She shivered, wishing she'd thought to bring a windbreaker. Todd and Jonathan piled wood for a small bonfire on a sandy scrap of shoreline.

After Todd lit the pile of wood, the flames reached upward, popping and cracking. At last the warmth reached her. Olivia stretched her hands toward the fire.

She and Jonathan had won second prize in the scavenger hunt, a tacky-looking pair of red plastic lobsters nearly a foot long apiece, along with a gift card for dinner at a local restaurant. Olivia sighed and dug her toes into the still-warm sand. Frances had called her bad news. All she really wanted to do was get on with her life instead of worry about what people thought about her.

"Warming up?" Jonathan eased onto the blanket next to her.

"Yes, some." Olivia raised hands to her hot face, and resisted the inclination to lean closer to Jonathan. He might have been her partner in the scavenger hunt, but she wasn't pairing off with him around the fire.

"Here." He tugged a windbreaker around her shoulders.

"Oh. Thanks. Are you sure you won't need it?"

"I'm fine. Borrowed it from Todd."

Olivia looked up to see Maggie and Todd, plus a guy from church carrying a guitar as they made their way on the winding path to the bonfire.

Three songs later, Olivia realized she and Jonathan sat cross-legged, shoulder to shoulder, arm to arm, and knee to knee. She'd practically drifted onto his lap. From his posture, he didn't look like he minded. She didn't want to move, but caught a knowing glance from Maggie.

Jonathan stood and stretched. "Maggie's got some marshmallows and sticks over there. Want some?"

"Sure." Olivia shifted to her original spot on the blanket, now cool from her absence. Jonathan brought back sticks impaled with several marshmallows.

She distracted herself by concentrating on her marshmallows, which ignited despite her attempt to ignore Jonathan's silhouette so near to her in the firelight. She laughed, pulled the stick from the fire and blew out the marshmallows.

"So…what are your plans after the summer's over?" Jonathan asked, his brown eyes gently probing.

"Well, the Cetacean Institute of Cape Ann has asked me to join their research department, pending my acceptance to the master's and doctorate program at UMass." Olivia tossed the charred remains of her marshmallows into the fire. "I'm submitting my application next week."

"Are you going to accept their offer?"

"Yes, I'm here to stay." Starting over was much different from picking up her old life where she left off.

Jonathan offered her one of his marshmallows. "I'm glad."

Olivia bit into the sticky sweetness. Some of the goo stuck to her chin. She tried to wipe it off with her fingers. "Thanks. It's the perfectly toasted marshmallow."

Her mind went blank when Jonathan cupped her chin with one hand and wiped the last of the marshmallow off with a roughened thumb. "There. You were just making things worse."

It was her turn to stand despite the dizzying sensations coursing through her. She wanted him to kiss her, and his eyes told her he wanted to do the same.

"I need to rinse my hands." Olivia headed away from the fire to the dark water spreading onto the wet sand. The water numbed her bare toes and swirled around her fingers as she squatted at the edge of the surf.

She sprang up before more water splashed up onto her shorts. With her wet fingers she cooled her hot cheeks. The salty water cleared her head and stilled the sensation of Jonathan's fingers on her chin. How could rough skin feel so soft? What had happened today to awaken something inside her, making her look at Jonathan—her old friend—as though he could be something more?

Loneliness. That could explain her reaction to Jonathan's attention. While in Pennsylvania, she hadn't thought about being alone. She'd kept busy and kept the past at bay as best she could. Now that she'd been home for a while, the past had reinserted itself into her life. But she could no longer insert herself into her old life here. The inky water drifted over her feet, the waves providing a soothing sound as they rolled over on themselves.

Olivia turned her back on the water to rejoin the others, dark shapes moving back and forth, blocking the glow of the fire.

"Lord, I'm lonely. I admit it. Please don't let me confuse friendship and kindness with anything more. It could hurt both of us." She trudged through the sand back to the blanket by the fire.

"So at the end of the month my cousin's heading out for another trip, maybe as far as the Grand Banks," the guitar player said. "Last time the lowest cut was close to five grand."

Jonathan whistled. "Good run."

"If you're looking into trawling, it's still a good living,

though not as much money as the swordfish boats. But then you probably know that." The man grinned and strummed a few chords.

"I don't mind." The firelight showed a gleam in Jonathan's eyes that Olivia hadn't seen in years. "I'm just looking to get out there again. Pete Celucci's selling his boat and I'm buying it."

"What?" Olivia sank to her knees as she stared at Jonathan. "What are you talking about?"

"I'm going out again. I've wanted it for a long time, and Pete's selling. I believe the Lord's given me another chance." Jonathan grinned, the ocean breeze ruffling his hair.

"You're right. He did." Olivia shivered under the jacket and slipped it from her shoulders. When Jonathan said nothing in response, she tossed her marshmallow roasting stick into the fire and rose. "Hey, Maggie, Todd, thanks for today. I had a great time, but I should go now. I might catch the fireworks on TV."

Maybe this was her answer to her whispered prayer. It was better she cut off any growing affection for Jonathan now before she ended up in the same heartache again. She snatched up her sneakers and socks, then jogged back to the house.

Chapter 5

Jonathan watched Olivia flee. What had happened to change her mood so suddenly? She'd responded when he swept the marshmallow from her chin. If he'd been more sure of himself and if things had been different, he'd have been glad to kiss the sweetness on her face. But now—

"What was that about?" His friend from church placed the guitar back in its case.

"I'm not quite sure, but I'll find out." Jonathan went after Olivia, wincing as he stubbed a toe on a rock. No way would he let her leave a wake of pavement behind her this time.

Olivia crossed the patio ahead of him and entered the kitchen. Jonathan caught up with her in the foyer. She was fumbling in her purse.

"Liv."

"What?" She clutched her car keys.

Jonathan reached for her free hand and rubbed the back of it with his thumb. "Getting my own rig is my dream, even after what happened with Robby. Don't look at me like that.

I'll say his name if I want to. You weren't the only one who lost someone."

"I know that." Her voice barely sounded above a whisper.

"Then be happy for me."

"But your carpentry."

"I can still do that. But it's important to me to get my business going again."

"Have you considered the risks?" She pulled her hand from his grasp.

"If there's anything I've learned, life is full of risks. We aren't guaranteed the next day or the next breath. But God's taking care of things for us." Jonathan reached for her shoulders, but she stepped back.

"Until the rug gets yanked out from under us on His whim." Her voice quavered.

"Liv, God's not like that."

"So you want to put yourself in danger again?"

"I'm not doing anything stupid. I know what I'm doing." How else could he make her understand? He was losing this round. Olivia backed away toward the front door. Jonathan let her go before frustration got the better of him and before she really lost her temper.

"Good night. See you at work." With that, the front door clicked shut.

He reentered the kitchen to find Todd and Maggie waiting for him. "Hey," was all he said.

"Olivia's gone?" Maggie asked.

Jonathan nodded. He saw the pair of plastic lobsters grinning at him from their perch on top of the microwave. She'd left their prize behind.

"She got upset when I mentioned buying Pete's boat."

Maggie frowned. "She's scared, Jonathan. Liv's done her best to be brave, coming back to Fairport."

"I know, but she grew up here. She knows what a fisherman's life is like." Why was he starting to feel like the bad guy all of a sudden?

Todd wrapped his arms around Maggie's shoulders. "Don't worry, she'll be fine."

Jonathan saw Maggie dart a look over her shoulder at her husband as she said, "Yes. And I still pray every time you head out, even on an all-day charter. We're only human, guys. We women try to be strong for our men and trust God with the rest." But she laid a hand on her belly.

"I know you do." Except he wasn't Olivia's man. Jonathan wandered to the microwave and picked up the lobsters. "Listen, I should probably get going. Work continues tomorrow, and there's this couple I know who want some bookcases finished."

They said their good-byes, and Jonathan left in his Jeep. Normally he'd stay until the last guest hit the road, but tonight he needed to drive. He wouldn't head to the apartment. Nothing waited for him there. His Jeep took him toward town, then down some side streets until it stopped in the parking lot of Safe Harbor Beach.

He crossed the walkway over the dune and faced the sea, the surf roaring the entire time. Like a magnet, the sea drew him closer. Just like seeing Olivia had drawn him to her again. Why now? Why were these feelings he had supposedly squelched years ago rising up?

"I don't understand, Lord. I'm acknowledging You in all my ways, and I believe Your Word says You'll direct me." Jonathan swallowed hard. "I also believe You've made a way for me to pursue my dream. I can hold my head high in town again. No more looks and silence when I walk into a room full of fishermen. No more feeling like I'm missing out. When would I get a chance like this again?"

Jonathan prayed a while longer. He wanted, no, needed this chance. At least he could pray and drive tonight. Now he needed to pray that Olivia would understand.

Olivia heard her father's snores before she opened the front door. She smiled in spite of her foul mood. The television was blaring the news, so she crossed the room to turn it down before waking her father.

"Dad." Olivia tugged on his big toe. "Dad, I'm home. Go on to bed."

Her father grunted, then shifted the recliner to an upright position. "You have a good time at Maggie's?"

"Yeah, I did."

"Huh," her father said. "So why do you look so mopey?"

She sank onto a nearby ottoman. "Jonathan said he's buying another boat."

"Yeah, I kinda figured that when I saw him shooting the breeze a couple weeks ago with Pete Celucci." Her father reached for the remote control and muted the TV. "Best thing that could happen to the boy."

"He was pretty happy about it." Olivia bit her lip. She was tired, and her head still hurt. Of course her father would understand Jonathan's point of view.

"And you're not happy."

She shrugged. "He said he was working on carpentry."

"All I can say is that the boy's born for the water. It goes way back in his family. Came here from Portugal a couple hundred years ago, even before we Sheas came from Ireland. If his dad's health wasn't so bad, he'd be up here instead of down in Florida year round."

"You see things his way because you're a fisherman, too." Her protest sounded feeble, petty to her ears. Of course Jonathan had a right to head for the ocean, to chase that dream again.

"Jonathan's a smart boy. He knows what he's doing." Her father's level gaze forced her to study the television screen where a woman was gesturing to a weather map.

"I know." Olivia sighed. "I'm just tired, and the news was a shock. I think I'll go to bed now." She headed up the stairs, the steps creaking.

Sleep refused to come when at last Olivia had changed into her nightshirt and crawled under the covers. She sighed, kicked off the blankets and found her Bible on the shelf. The Psalms always brought comfort to her. No one else seemed to understand her feelings at the moment.

Olivia turned the pages until they stopped at chapter 46. *"God is our refuge and strength, a present help in time of trouble. Though the mountains shake in the heart of the sea, though the oceans roar and foam, we will not fear."* So she shouldn't be afraid. God would be her strength and her refuge. Then why didn't she feel strong and secure? Jonathan had every right to want his dream back. She had no business telling him what he ought or ought not to do. Why did the fear keep trying to wrap her in its tentacles and smother her like some great underwater beast? Had the psalmist ever felt the earth give way beneath him, or felt the fury of the ocean?

She finished reading the chapter, hoping to pull some reassurance from the sacred words. Tears pricked her eyes.

"Father God, I'm sorry. I've tried to trust You before, and look what happened. It didn't work. You…You let me down. How do I know it won't happen again?" Olivia closed the leather cover and set the Bible on her desk instead of on the shelf.

Out went the light, and the darkness seemed tangible. She slipped back in bed for another attempt at sleep. Lights from the street below flickered with passing cars. The television, now back to its former volume, bellowed about the concert earlier that evening with the Boston Pops. Olivia stared at the ceiling, then gasped.

She'd left her lobster at Maggie's. Jonathan must really think her a heel now. And she had to face him at the boat come morning. Some friend she was.

The four-day work week should have felt shorter, but time on the boat dragged for Jonathan. Olivia barely spoke to him except when necessary. What could he say to calm her fear? Part of him wondered how much she cared for him if she seemed to worry so much. Could it be that maybe a chance remained they could someday be more than friends?

By Friday he'd had enough of the silence. With Maggie's prize lobster perched on the seat next to him, Jonathan drove to the Sheas' house. He'd finished Todd and Maggie's bookcases last night and delivered the set to their house. The pride of his accomplishment, plus Maggie's encouragement that Olivia had cooled off, boosted his confidence to bring the lobster as a peace offering.

An express delivery truck blocked the Sheas' driveway, so Jonathan parked behind Olivia's car on the street. The silly lobster grinned at him as he grabbed it from the front seat. "Here goes, Smiley. If I get shot down, so do you."

Jonathan nodded to the departing deliveryman, and pounded up the front steps. Good. The screen door was open.

Sam answered his knock. "Jonathan, c'mon in. You get to be the first to see my new toy." He appeared to study the lobster in Jonathan's hands.

"Toy?" Jonathan tucked the lobster under one arm and opened the screen door. He followed Sam to the living room.

Olivia was kneeling beside a box printed with the name of a mega-computer firm. She shook her head, glossy brown hair streaming past her shoulders. Jonathan liked her hair down. Had she been growing it longer this summer? His palms felt damp around the plastic creature in his hands.

"Dad, I'm shocked. I'm proud of you. Your own computer…" Her voice trailed off when she looked up and Jonathan held out the lobster.

"Hi. Smiley's missed you." He waved it at her.

A flicker of humor sparked in her eyes. "He has?"

He nodded, taking a seat on the floor across from her while Sam settled into his easy chair. "He's been hanging around the house with Thelma all week." Jonathan couldn't believe he was discussing plastic lobsters and naming them in front of Olivia's father, no less.

"Poor guy. Welcome home, Smiley." Olivia gave the lobster a pat and put him on the coffee table. "Wait there while I open this computer."

"I decided it was about time I get modernized here," Sam's voice boomed. "You ever use computers, Jon?"

"Some." Jonathan watched Olivia carefully unpack a monitor, along with a keyboard and speakers.

"My sister down in Boston was nagging me to get online, so I figure this old dog can learn some new things." Sam chuckled.

Olivia stood, clutching the monitor. "Dad, where do you want this set up? Your old desk in the entryway? Or do you want to have one built? I know this guy who's a good carpenter."

"The desk in the entryway's fine."

Jonathan followed Olivia to the entryway and watched her set the monitor on the cluttered desk. How in the world did Sam keep everything straight? At least they wouldn't have to move the mammoth piece of furniture. Its broad surface would leave plenty of room for the computer. Sam had ordered one of those all-in-one computers. Nice.

Olivia sighed, shoving papers out of the way, and set the monitor down in the middle of the desk. "All right. Give me a few minutes, and I'll have you hooked up. Are you sure there's a plug behind this desk?"

"The lamp's plugged into the wall back there."

She fed the cables through the space between the desk and the wall. "Now, all I have to do is get under here to plug everything in."

She crawled under the desk. "Dad, you really need to clean behind the desk." Her voice sounded muffled. "It's a fire hazard with all this paper down here... Hold on, I found the plugs."

Sam looked at Jonathan with hopeful eyes. "Hope this works. Say, you got plans for supper?"

"No."

"Well, stay, then. I'm sure Liv will make enough for all of us, won't you, Liv?"

The cords had stopped their wiggling between the top of the desk and the wall. Olivia hadn't emerged from under the desk.

"Liv?" Sam ducked his head down.

Olivia scooted backward on her hands and knees. She stood, tossing crumpled papers and a wrinkled envelope onto the desk. Then she sneezed.

"What's wrong?" Jonathan glanced at the small pile of papers.

"Look at the envelope." Her face had blanched.

Jonathan picked up the letter-sized envelope, first noting the Fairport postmark, then the return address. Sent from Robby O'Leary to Olivia Shea, the letter was postmarked the same day the *Lady Jane* had shipped out two years ago, never to return.

Chapter 6

Olivia stared at the envelope. "Dad."

"Go ahead." Pop placed a hand on her shoulder, and its warm strength did battle with her pounding heart. "You read it. Jonathan and I'll see to supper." The hand lifted. Heavy steps left the entryway.

She didn't venture to meet Jonathan's eyes. "Did you know?"

He drew a ragged breath. "Yeah, I knew Robby had written you a letter."

Olivia reached for the envelope. "I'll go read it." At last she glanced at him. Their fingers touched, a gentle pressure through the paper as Jonathan kept her hand in his. Shadowed eyes revealed nothing. His stubble of beard made him appear older and tired.

She wanted him to smile for her, to reassure her that this letter would serve to remind her of the special place Robby once had in her life. Yet a gnawing began in her stomach.

Stop it. What harm could it be, reading a letter written by a dead man? But what did Robby have to tell her that he needed to put in a letter? He'd never been given to letter writing.

"I'll be here." He released her hand and the letter. Her hand felt cold without his touch.

Olivia turned and climbed the stairs to her room. Shutting the door with a firm click, she settled onto her bed. Should she rip into the envelope? Or should she open it carefully to respect Robby's memory? And what would she want to do with the letter after reading its contents?

Within seconds, the letter lay unfolded on her lap. Olivia filled her lungs with air, then began to read:

Dear Liv,

Tomorrow I head out for another month. But I can't leave without telling you how much you mean to me. You're a wonderful young woman with a bright future ahead of you.

I think we should call off the wedding and step back to take a look at things. For the past year it's been all you've talked about and focused on. You need to make sure you're going to be happy spending your life waiting for a guy like me to come home to you all the time. After the wedding, it's back to the same old, same old.

I don't want you feeling like you settled for less than God's best for you. I know God watches over us, but we never know when we will lose loved ones. I couldn't bear leaving you if I knew you'd spent your life loving me more than anything else.

I hope you understand. I love you, but I don't want you missing out on something better. If you need help with the wedding stuff, ask Mom. I know she'll help out canceling orders. We'll talk more when I get back.
Love,
Robby

He'd wanted to call off the wedding? How could Robby have thought she'd be settling?

The words squeaked out. "I can't believe it." Olivia flopped onto her back.

How ironic. Olivia remembered she had indeed canceled the caterer, the musicians, the florist. Frances had been too numb after the shipwreck to offer much help, although while planning the wedding Frances had tried to push her own ideas until Olivia was ready to scream.

She also remembered she'd closed herself off and shut down her emotions when Robby's boat was lost. She hadn't even cried at the memorial service. When a young woman had needed a wedding gown in a hurry, Olivia had given her the dress without a qualm. She no longer felt attached to a dream dress that she would never wear.

What difference would it have made if she'd found it back when his boat was lost? Would she have even left Fairport and tried to start a new life?

She rolled onto her stomach, burying her face in the comforter, inhaling the scent of fabric softener.

"What does he mean that I was so focused on the wedding for that whole year? How dare he?" She had done everything a good fisherman's woman was supposed to do. She'd waited, she'd prayed. She hadn't complained. What else was there for her to do besides work on her degrees and plan a wedding?

She sat up, glaring at the paper on the floor. Robby had made her sound as if she'd been smothering him and had been superficial for focusing on their wedding. Of course, all brides were caught up in the moment. Olivia shook her head. He'd wanted to postpone the wedding.

Not that it mattered now.

"So what will it be? Pot roast or meat loaf? I'm throwing a stir-fry dinner in the microwave for Liv." Sam's thick upper torso was hidden behind the freezer door, but the top of his shaggy gray head appeared over the top.

"Pot roast." Jonathan watched the older man open the frozen dinner boxes.

By the time the meals were heated through, Jonathan learned more than he thought he'd ever want to know about lobstering. Sam Shea had to be lonely. Never had he heard the fisherman say so much in one stretch of time.

His thoughts remained with Liv upstairs. On the *Lady Jane*'s last trip Robby had mentioned he'd come to some decisions on their relationship.

"Here you are." Sam slid the pot roast dinner onto a plate. "Guess we'll eat now. Liv will come down when she's ready."

Jonathan was halfway through his meal when he heard Olivia's footsteps on the stairs. Sam continued to eat as though he'd heard nothing.

Olivia's smile warmed his heart, but her blotchy cheeks made his gut tighten. "Are you all right?"

"I'll be okay." She glanced at her father, then took her seat at the weathered table.

"Your dinner's in the oven. I gave you the stir fry," Sam said around a mouthful.

"Thanks." After sitting down with her meal, Liv bowed her head briefly, then picked up her fork. "Robby sent the letter because he wanted to call off the wedding…indefinitely." Her brown eyes glistened as she took a bite of rice.

Jonathan had clenched a hand into a fist before he realized it. He'd let Sam speak first. The older man chewed his bite, not looking up from his plate.

If Jonathan had Robby here right now, he'd be tempted to slug the guy. Robby never had gotten around to saying what he'd decided about Liv. What had changed Robby's mind? Liv could be a little intense sometimes, but her passion for life had always appealed to Jonathan.

Even after taking a sip of his iced tea, Jonathan waited for Sam to speak. But maybe Robby hadn't really wanted to marry Olivia at all. The thought struck him like a punch.

Jonathan recalled the morning Robby had announced the

engagement. The two of them were hosing down the deck of the *Lady Jane*.

"Liv's wanting to get married, so I went ahead and asked her," was what Robby had said. "She didn't come out and say it, but I could tell."

From that point on, Olivia had run the show. Even at the time, Jonathan had told Robby he should have made more of an effort with the proposal. Cold feet, indeed.

The sound of Olivia's voice jolted him back.

"I'm sorry, what were you saying?"

"Did you know Robby was calling off the wedding? You said you knew about the letter." Her voice sounded hard.

"No. I didn't know he'd said that." Jonathan refused to tear his gaze from hers. "Robby said he'd made some decisions about the relationship, but he never got the chance to tell me." He unclenched his fist, wanting nothing more than to move to Olivia's side of the table and take her in his arms.

Sam sighed. "It's a shock, and it's a shame. I'd be lying if I said I wouldn't want to knock some sense into Robby if I could right about now." He patted Olivia's hand. "But what's done is done. Can't go back. All you can do is go ahead."

"Thanks, Dad. You're right. And Jon, I'm glad you're here." Olivia focused on her supper.

Sam pushed back from the table. "Of course we're here for you. I'm going to put my plate in the sink and catch the news, and let you young people be. I'm sure you've got some things to talk about."

What an understatement. Jonathan took the last bite of his meal.

After they cleared the dishes from the table, Liv refilled their iced tea glasses. Jonathan took that as a hint for him to stay.

"Do you want to sit on the porch? Dad and I like to go out there some evenings." Her eyes looked like sweet chocolate.

"Sure." His palms had gone sweaty again, but it was probably because of the wet glass.

The July sun was swiftly disappearing to the west, lighting the street in a midsummer glow. A salty breeze drifted through the air. Jonathan would never tire of the smell.

They sat side by side on the ancient porch swing, just like Olivia and Robby had sat side by side after they'd started seeing each other long ago. Jonathan remembered leaving earlier after supper back then. He'd felt like a fifth wheel.

"You doing better?"

Olivia nodded.

"Good."

Then she sighed. "I just…"

"What?"

"I just wonder if I was as all-consumed by the wedding as Robby said I was…and so totally focused on him that I didn't see anyone or anything else." She sipped her tea, then let the ice cubes swirl around the glass.

Jonathan wanted to choose his words carefully. "Does it matter now?"

"No, not really. I just wonder if I knew him as well as I thought I did. He seemed excited to be getting married." Olivia studied her tea glass. "I mean, aren't grooms supposed to be?"

"Uh, I would guess so." Jonathan cleared his throat. "I mean, it's not like some of the stuff women worry about is a big deal to us guys."

"True. I know that. He fell asleep one night here on the couch when I was showing him bridesmaids' dress ideas." Olivia smiled, then laughed. "I guess I did obsess a little."

But Robby had been almost nonchalant about the proposal and everything. A man shouldn't be nonchalant concerning the woman he loved. Jonathan pondered that for a moment. He didn't see the point in bringing *that* up now.

"What?" She nudged him. "What aren't you telling me?"

Jonathan shrugged. "He just didn't seem that gung ho about getting married. I shouldn't say anything. It doesn't really matter much now, not that either one of us can do anything about it."

"Not gung ho about getting married?" Olivia shook her head. "I know he was pretty laid-back about many things, but..." She sealed her lips into a thin line.

"I'm sorry. I shouldn't have said anything. Robby was a good man and he did love you."

"Just not enough, apparently."

Jonathan sighed. Here was the chance he'd once longed for, and a chance he'd surrendered when he saw the sparks fly between Robby and Olivia years ago. Physical romance didn't necessarily guarantee commitment and a lot of couples skipped that commitment.

He reached out, touched her silken hair.

Olivia could hardly form her words at the sensations bubbling inside her at the mere caress of Jonathan's hand to her hair. His dark features were inches from her head, the rough stubble on his face begged her to touch it.

Then he put his glass down and she was able to breathe again. She followed suit, glad to put the glass in a safe place. If she were any more distracted she'd drop it.

"What is it?" Jonathan settled back onto the swing, this time settling his arm around her shoulder.

She shook her head. She wouldn't fall apart in front of him. Then the warmth of his arm was behind her again, and Olivia leaned into its security. She sniffed.

"Go ahead," his husky voice whispered, inches from her left ear.

"What?"

"Cry. I know I did."

Olivia sat upright and stared at him. "Jonathan...I..."

Jonathan turned to face her, offering her a place in the circle of his arms. Olivia accepted the invitation, burying her face in his shoulder. He smelled of the sea and aftershave.

A sob made Olivia shudder, but Jonathan's arms around her told her she was safe. For the first time since the evening of the storm, Olivia felt like she had her old friend back. Except the old friendship was carried on a current of something new. She felt her shoulders tense.

"What is it?" Jonathan stroked her hair with one hand.

"I'm not sure how to say this." Olivia shifted to her place on the swing. What if she opened her mouth and said the wrong thing, and the sweetness of this healing moment was lost?

"Hey, it's me here. We've known each other a long time." Jonathan left his arm around her.

"I know. And that's why I'm afraid, but I'll say it anyway. I feel like something's happening between us. And I don't know what to do about it."

"Don't worry about it. If God is circling our paths closer together, then so be it." Then his smile lit the early evening, its shine affecting her the way no glow of fireflies could ever do.

Now Jonathan was close enough so she could feel his breath on her face. What would it be like to have him kiss her? She resisted the urge to lick her lips. A strong hand caught her around the waist, pulling her still closer.

The porch light clicked on, and Olivia blinked. Her father stuck his head out the door.

"Er, I'm heading upstairs now. Make sure you lock up." Then he gave Jonathan a nod before closing the door.

Olivia released her breath and giggled. "What timing."

Jonathan stood and stretched, then took her hand and pulled her to her feet. "Ah, Miss Shea, if I kissed you now, I'd scratch your face."

Olivia wanted to reply that a scratched face was the least of her concerns. "And?"

"When I do kiss you, I'll make sure I've shaved first." Then he winked at her, fishing his keys from his pocket. "I need to leave now. Morning comes early."

"Oh. Right." Olivia mustered a feeble wave as Jonathan climbed into his Jeep and left.

Jonathan turned the corner and groaned. What had happened back there? All he'd done was show up with a plastic lobster, and nearly ended the evening sharing a kiss with Olivia. Smiley had turned into quite a peace offering. He allowed himself a grin at that.

No, it was Robby's stupid letter. If Olivia hadn't found that letter, none of them would have known about Robby's decision to call off the wedding. Then he wouldn't have ended up comforting Olivia on the porch.

"Dummy." Jonathan glared at his reflection in the rearview mirror. He hoped he hadn't crossed any unmarked lines tonight. Having the chance to comfort Olivia and encourage her was an answer to a prayer. Yet where did friendship end and something more begin?

"Okay, Barrotta. She's a grown woman. She could have pushed you away." Jonathan pulled into the parking space at his apartment. Yet Olivia hadn't pushed him away. Her expressive eyes had practically begged him to kiss her. It was probably just as well her father had opened the front door when he did.

That night, he bowed in prayer in his bedroom. "Help me, Lord. You know how much I've cared for her all these years. Please don't let me take advantage of her needing comfort. You do the comforting and healing, and I'll be there for her when You're through. I promise You that. If You're giving me a chance to love her at last."

Chapter 7

Olivia hummed while she whisked the waffle batter in a bowl and smelled the coffee streaming into the coffeepot. She heard her father descend the creaking stairs, his slippers swishing on the wood. The swish paused, then came the whir of the computer. Olivia smiled. Her father was checking his email, a new tradition blending with the old.

To think a computer would come before her father's trip to the porch step for the morning paper. But then laughter came more easily than it had for a long time.

Two weeks and three days had passed since Jonathan nearly kissed her on the porch swing. Maybe he would sometime. Her stomach trembled at the thought.

Since that night, her heart had poured out the accumulated sludge of old feelings and hurts. On a sunny Sunday morning like this, the past seemed like an old nightmare chased forever back into the shadows. Now that she and Jonathan had reestablished their friendship, she realized she'd welcome more.

"Yes, Lord," she murmured. "I want Your best for Jonathan, and for me. If You want us to be together, I'll accept that. Please, show us Your will." Jonathan's dark curly hair, deep brown eyes, his stubbled jaw when he forgot to shave all sprang to mind. Olivia sighed and rested her elbows on the counter, feeling like a schoolgirl again.

The scent of burning waffles filled the air. Olivia jerked the cover from the waffle iron. Steam swirled up, revealing dark brown squares.

Her father scuffed into the kitchen. "You planning on feeding me that?" He sniffed the air, reading glasses perched on the end of his nose.

"You can put lots of syrup on it. Wait, too much isn't very good for you. Or margarine for that matter." Olivia waved the spatula she used to pry the burned mass from the waffle iron. She tossed the waffles in the trash and put fresh batter in the waffle iron.

Her father helped himself to the coffee, then coughed before he took a sip.

"Dad, are you okay?"

"I'm fine. Just a summer cold."

"Ever since I've been home? That's a long cold." She wouldn't bring up the pipe tobacco.

"Like I said, I'm fine." He spread the newspaper out on the table. With a grunt, Olivia's father turned to the Sports section of the Boston paper.

"Will you come to church this morning? Pastor's been asking about you." Olivia braced herself for the reply.

"Tell him I'm doing great." He set his coffee mug on the table with a thunk. "Business is so good, I need to rest and catch up on work around the house."

"All right." The light blinked on the waffle iron. Olivia placed the steaming waffles on two plates, then brought them to the table.

When she was a child, her father would drop her off at church and pick her up afterward. Either that or he'd let her go with Mrs. Flaherty next door. Why wouldn't he come with her? Why the need to stay away?

"I love God in my own way. I don't need to show up to please people...." His voice trailed off.

Olivia wouldn't argue with him there she thought as she ate her breakfast. After Robby died, she had longed for the sanctuary of God's house, but she couldn't deal with curious glances and vague whispers and too-bright smiles. So she'd stopped attending altogether until she moved to Pennsylvania.

Except Jonathan would nod at her, giving her a slight smile that didn't mask the sorrow in his eyes. He had been through the valley of the shadow of death and come through alive. He understood. What must that be like for him?

She brushed aside the somber thoughts and silently toasted the bright morning with her cup of coffee.

"I don't know if some of the gang will go out to lunch or not, but I'll call you if we do so you won't wait for me."

Olivia's father grunted again in response and patted her shoulder as she left the table.

Maggie settled onto the chair next to her in Sunday school.

"Hey, guess what?" Maggie beamed. But then she always beamed lately.

"What?"

"Todd's mom gave me a gift certificate to the Children's Orchard! She knew I'd be wanting to get a head start on shopping for the baby."

Olivia managed a grin for her friend. "Let me guess. You couldn't wait for a baby shower. That gift certificate's probably burning a hole in your purse."

"Shopping trip? In Newburyport?"

"Sounds great!" She needed a diversion from Jonathan, from her paperwork-gathering for graduate school. A shopping trip would do the trick.

Jeremy, their teacher, called the class to order and opened in prayer. "Now, let's look at the first lesson in the quarterly journal. I know you haven't had a chance to study it, but I figured we could start today as an introduction."

Olivia read the title of the lesson. "Calming the Storm." Was this a conspiracy? She'd been sailing through a hurricane, thunderstorm and tornado all at once it seemed.

A sideways glance at Jonathan showed brown eyes probing her for a reaction. Olivia set her jaw. She wouldn't let him, wouldn't let anyone see her reaction to the upcoming lecture.

Olivia had heard the story from childhood, of Jesus sleeping inside the boat during the storm, while the disciples panicked. She remembered giggling with the rest of the class. Silly disciples. Scared to pieces while the Son of God accompanied them across the lake in a storm.

Then she had grown up. Adult fear had replaced her child's faith.

Jeremy continued. "Note that in Mark 4:35, Jesus tells the disciples they are going to the other side. I'm sure He knew a storm was coming, that their very lives would be in danger. The lesson asks an interesting question on page three: Why do you think the disciples allowed fear to overcome them? Anyone care to answer?"

"They were human," someone called out.

"Good," said Jeremy.

Olivia could understand the disciples' feelings. Wasn't fear a human reaction to a threatening event?

Then Jonathan spoke up. "They let their circumstances and present surroundings affect them more than the words of Jesus."

Ouch. For some reason Olivia's chair felt more uncomfortable than usual this morning. She took a sip of coffee and doodled a design in the margin of her lesson book.

"That's true, Jonathan. When we find ourselves in threatening or uncertain conditions, it's easy to forget the words that the Lord has for us. Right here." Jeremy held up his leather-bound Bible.

Olivia kept doodling, concentrating on her design. She'd

read the Bible before, and even knew some verses from memory. Had her mind merely memorized the words? Had the knowledge penetrated to her heart?

The whisper of turning pages grabbed her attention. "Oh, where are we turning to now?" She glanced at Jonathan's Bible, where he'd flipped to Romans 8.

"Beth, could you read verses thirty-five, then thirty-seven through thirty-nine, please?" Jeremy asked.

"Who shall separate us from the love of Christ? Shall tribulation, or distress, or persecution, or famine, or nakedness, or peril, or sword?

"Yet in all these things we are more than conquerors through him who loved us.

"For I am persuaded that neither death, nor life, nor angels nor principalities nor powers, nor things present nor things to come, nor height nor depth, nor any other created thing shall be able to separate us from the love of God which is in Christ Jesus our Lord."

Olivia kept focusing on the lesson's theme. If the Bible said nothing on this earth could keep Olivia from God's love, why did she feel so unconvinced? Had her fear and possessiveness caused hurt to those around her? If she had been less possessive and fearful about Robby, would he still be here today? No, that wouldn't have changed the outcome.

Olivia felt a weight pressing down on the back of her chair. Jonathan's arm brushed her shoulders. Normally the sensation would have comforted her.

She didn't deserve Jonathan's comfort. Not when the very words that should have helped her made her feel worse than before.

Chapter 8

Olivia touched a soft cotton blanket woven in pastel colors. She'd driven with Maggie riding shotgun, and now they were in a baby furniture store just over the New Hampshire line.

"No sales tax," Maggie had said with a mischievous grin.

One day, Olivia wanted to go through the whole process. What would it be like to finally be married and start a family? She'd made some relationship mistakes in the past. She'd let Robby be the main focus of her life. Even above the Lord. Olivia swallowed hard at the realization that Robby had been right. It wasn't just being a wedding-crazy woman or her natural grief over losing him. She'd made him her rock when he was only a man.

"I said, what do you think of this? Do you think it'll be too dark for the nursery?" Maggie lovingly stroked an elegant sleigh-bed crib of cherrywood.

"I'm sorry, I was thinking."

"Yeah, I could tell. So what else do you think? If you had to buy a crib for the nursery, which one would you choose?"

That was easy. A rich maple crib, with wood tones warm enough to complement any style of crib bedding. Couldn't she imagine standing at its edge, looking down at a sleeping infant with dark licorice hair curling over his head, just like his father's?

"This one here." Olivia's cheeks flamed at her musings.

Maggie joined her at the piece of furniture. "Yeah, this is beautiful. You're right. I like this even better than the other piece." She flipped over the price tag. "Ouch, that hurts. But I have an idea."

Olivia nodded absently. How could she be thinking of Jonathan now? And what would he think if he knew her thoughts? No more jumping headlong into another relationship. This time she'd go in with eyes open, slow and wary.

Maggie held up her phone and snapped a picture of the crib. "I'm going to see if Todd thinks we can afford having Jonathan make it. He's a genius with wood. But I guess you know that."

"That's right. I was hoping to have him make Dad a new computer desk for his birthday or even Christmas."

They wandered toward the women's clothing department. Maggie continued her probing.

"So, I'm sure you know Jonathan's not planning to stay in woodworking permanently." Maggie held up a pair of baby shoes.

"Oh, those are cute! Too bad these aren't in grown-up sizes." Olivia reached for the shoes.

"You're avoiding my question."

"Yes." Olivia ran her fingers over the supple leather. "I do know Jonathan's plans, and I'm scared for him. I think if he keeps at his woodworking, he could open his own shop."

"What if that's not what he really wants? Or what if it's not what God has for him?"

Olivia sighed. "I suppose it's pointless to tell you how I feel."

Maggie frowned and reached for another pair of shoes. "Yeah, I've been there. Many of the women in town have been there. Lots of us have been fortunate. Some haven't. It's a tough life, but I do know I would never deny Todd his dream."

Olivia nodded. Which was why if Jonathan wanted to go out on a fishing boat again, she wouldn't stop him. Olivia would guard her heart. She would do things right this time.

They stopped for lunch at a courtyard café. Olivia lingered over her strawberry pie. Maggie would get a break from walking, whether she wanted one or not. The town's summer hubbub of tourists and shoppers flowed past them.

"Oof. Maybe I shouldn't have eaten that dessert." Maggie frowned as she rubbed her stomach.

"Are you okay?"

"I'm fine." She took a sip of water. "Ow."

As they waited for their bill, Olivia hoped the pains would subside, but instead they grew stronger the longer they sat. Olivia wasn't sure what to expect, but Maggie didn't seem fine to her.

"I should call Todd." Olivia's heart started to beat faster.

"No! He didn't want me to go shopping today, not really."

Olivia turned on her cell phone. "I'm calling Todd anyway."

Maggie took a deep, slow breath. "Ow, these must be Braxton-Hicks contractions. But I think it's too early."

The answering machine came on at Todd's fishing charter office. Olivia gave her cell phone number, and asked him to call as soon as possible. She glanced at Maggie, whose white knuckles clenched a paper napkin. "Who else can I call?"

"Call my OB. The number's in my wallet."

Olivia found a business card for the obstetrics office and dialed. "Yes, I understand." Olivia hung up the phone. "We need to drive you to the hospital. Your doctor is contacting Labor and Delivery there. They'll be waiting for us."

Maggie clenched her stomach and bit her lip. Olivia laid some cash on the table with their bill. Her heart thudded and the world moved in slow motion. Be strong for Maggie. Maggie needed her. *Lord, help her. Help me.*

* * *

They arrived at the hospital, where an orderly met them and wheeled Maggie to the Labor and Delivery floor. *Don't let us be too late. Protect Maggie's little one.*

"Please, let my friend come with me. We haven't reached my husband yet." Maggie pleaded with the nurses.

Maggie had Olivia's hand in a vise grip as they wheeled her into an examining room. A woman in a white coat held some papers and attached them to a clipboard. Olivia managed to get away from Maggie and used a hall phone to try Todd. Still no answer.

She bit her lip, then dialed Jonathan's number.

"You're home!" Olivia nearly shrieked with relief when he answered.

"What's wrong? What's going on?"

"I need you to find Todd ASAP. I just brought Maggie to the hospital. She's having bad pains. I hope it's not early labor."

"I'll find him. We'll be there."

"I can't keep my cell phone on here in the hospital, but here's my number anyway. I've got voice mail."

"I'll call the emergency prayer group from church."

"Thanks."

Just hearing Jonathan's firm voice had calmed her somewhat. When she reentered the room, an attendant was performing a sonogram. Maggie's white face and round-eyed expression beckoned to her. A monitor displayed the baby's heartbeat along with Maggie's vitals.

Olivia took Maggie's hand. "It's going to be okay. Jonathan's going to find Todd and come with him."

"My baby. God, please, let me keep my baby." Tears pooled in Maggie's eyes.

"Excuse me." A nurse came to Maggie's side. "I need to get your blood pressure."

Olivia stepped back, winding her purse strap around a fin-

ger. She shouldn't have encouraged Maggie to make this trip.
She hadn't been this afraid since—

She started to pray more fervently. *Lord, help them hurry.*

Jonathan accompanied Todd to the hospital. He'd heard
the fear in Olivia's voice, and he wanted to be there for her as
much as for Todd and Maggie. Olivia met them in the waiting
room, her sweet chocolate eyes filled with worry and relief.

"The doctor's examining her now," Olivia told Todd, then
surprised Jonathan with a quick embrace. She left an arm
around his waist. "I'm glad you're here."

"Thanks, Liv. If you hadn't been here—" Todd squeezed
her elbow.

"Thank God I was. And I'm glad Jonathan found you."

"I'm going to see my wife now. I'd appreciate your prayers."

Jonathan nodded. He liked the way Olivia leaned on him.
He slid his arm around her shoulders. "Do you want to wait
for a while? Would you like that?"

"Yes, I want to know they'll both be okay."

The door opened and the ultrasound attendant wheeled the
cart down the hall. Jonathan released Olivia as she moved to
sit on a cushioned chair.

The hospital traffic swirled around them, women in various
stages of pregnancy coming and going. Some with a spouse,
others alone or with a friend. A young couple walked the
hallway, the husband murmuring encouragement to his wife.

Jonathan hoped one day that would be him. He wanted as
many kids as the Lord would bless him and his future wife
with. How many children did Olivia want? She was an only
child. He had grown up in an active noisy family of three boys.
But what was he thinking? Olivia had kept a cautious distance from him lately, although her hug had encouraged him.

At last Todd emerged from an exam room. "Hey, you two.
Thanks for waiting. The doctor wants to keep Maggie for
a while longer, probably overnight. She's not bleeding, but

because of her history they want to watch her and the baby carefully."

"That sounds better, man." Jonathan stood and clapped Todd on the back. "You're staying with her, right?"

"Yeah. Chuck's got the charter scheduled tomorrow anyway."

"I'll call the shop and let them know you won't be back." He followed Todd to the exam room doorway. Olivia passed them both and entered the room ahead of them.

Jonathan peeked inside. Maggie was whispering to Olivia. With a swirl of brown hair, Olivia bent to hug her friend.

She faced Jonathan. "Are you ready to leave?"

He nodded.

The late-summer evening air caused little goose bumps to form on Olivia's arms. Tomorrow's duties clamored for attention, but Jonathan kept focused on the silent woman beside him.

"You hangin' in there?" He put a protective arm around her as they walked to her car.

"Yes. I wish I hadn't encouraged her to go on this shopping trip."

"C'mon now. You know it's not your fault. Keeping Maggie from a good sale is like trying to keep the tide from coming in. It's not gonna happen."

For the first time since he'd seen her at the hospital, a smile flickered across Olivia's face. "That's true." She laughed. "We did find some good sales. Most of the stuff in the trunk is Maggie's."

Really. He didn't know how the two women did it. Sort of like sharks smelling blood, the way those two honed in on sales.

Then Olivia's smile faded. "Todd mentioned something about Maggie's history. What did he mean by that?"

Jonathan swallowed hard. "I assumed you knew. Maggie had a miscarriage before this pregnancy."

* * *

"Miscarriage?" Olivia felt her stomach drop to her feet. "I—I had no idea." Why hadn't Maggie told her?

Jonathan sighed. "About eight months ago."

And all that time Olivia had been in Pennsylvania, nursing her selfish hurts; she'd turned tail and ran. Fresh shame surged through her heart.

"Oh, that's horrible. I can't imagine what they must be going through. No wonder she was so frightened. I mean—to lose a child—" Olivia's throat ached.

"We just need to keep praying and entrust them to the Lord. It's all we can do."

Jonathan sounded so sure of himself. Entrust her friends and their unborn child to the Lord's care. "Sometimes that's easier said than done." She swallowed the lump and felt tears stinging her eyes.

"But it can be done." Jonathan's firm voice sounded low to her ears. "He wouldn't have asked us to cast our cares upon Him if it were impossible."

They headed into the north end of Fairport and Olivia decided to broach a safe subject. "I'd like to see if you could build a computer desk for Dad's birthday."

"Sure, I'll do it, time permitting." Jonathan faced the window. Olivia couldn't see the expression in his dark eyes.

"I could find a pattern. Or we could go to one of those home improvement warehouses and you could help me pick out wood. I wouldn't know what to choose." Olivia knew she had started babbling. A car almost cut them off in the traffic, so she eased off the accelerator and fastened her gaze straight ahead.

"That sounds great to me. I've decided to cut back on my carpentry projects for now, but for you, I'll do the desk."

Olivia smiled. "Thanks." He was going back on the boats. Probably with Pete Celucci. Of course he was. She should be happy for him. And part of her was.

Olivia crossed the short bridge over the inlet into Fairport and maneuvered through the narrow streets. Home. The lights in the harbor twinkled. A lighthouse at the edge of the harbor winked at them. The serene coastline helped to calm Olivia's tumbled thoughts.

Jonathan punctuated the silence. "Thanks for the ride."

"No problem. Thanks for going to the hospital." She turned onto Todd and Maggie's street, following the winding road that paralleled the shore. "Is Todd going to call you?"

"Yeah. He said he'd call me in the morning. I'm holding the fort for him at the shop until he and Maggie get back."

Gravel crunched under the car's tires. Olivia pulled into the driveway and stopped behind Jonathan's Jeep, then shifted into Park. Silence loomed between them in the front seat.

"You're a good friend to drop what you're doing for them. I'm—I'm glad you came with Todd." Olivia bit her lip at the admission.

"I would have done the same for you. Drop what I'm doing, if you needed me."

They'd been through so much together, Olivia didn't doubt it. "I know. I'm sorry my mouth ran away with me tonight. I know what you're saying is the truth, about trusting God to care for my friends."

"I tell you the truth because I care for you."

Olivia glanced in Jonathan's direction at the sound of his voice. Did his voice suddenly catch? Did his eyes suddenly seem shinier in the streetlight? Then his gaze flicked toward his Jeep.

"I know." Now her voice caught in her throat.

"Just remember, 'God is our refuge and strength, a present help in time of trouble.'"

"'Though the mountains shake in the heart of the sea, though the oceans roar and foam, we will not fear.' Yes, I've read that psalm." Olivia rubbed her forehead, which had started to ache.

"I want you to have some peace in your heart, Liv."

"I know." Her throat ached, the words barely escaping her lips.

"Well, it's getting late. Are you going to be okay?"

Now it was Olivia's turn to look away. "For tonight I will be."

"I'll call you if I hear anything."

"Thanks."

He leaned over and kissed her cheek. "G'night, Liv."

Her face burned where his lips had touched her. "Good night."

Chapter 9

"I'm so embarrassed." Maggie sounded sheepish on the phone.

"Are you okay? How's the baby?" Olivia wanted to reach through the line and hug her.

"I'm fine, and she's fine."

"Do they know what was wrong?"

Her heart started to pound with Maggie's silence.

"Yeah, they decided it was, um, the ham-and-egg break-fast bagel I had yesterday morning. I had gas."

"Whew. That's good. I mean, it's not good you hurt so bad." Olivia sighed.

"But Todd and the doctor want me to stop working now, and that includes going to the lab at the institute. And I have to agree with them."

"I'll miss you. I start back Monday full time. But I know Todd's thinking of your health and the baby." She didn't mention the miscarriage.

Maggie chuckled. "He's treated me like a porcelain doll

ever since I got home earlier this morning. He wouldn't even let me empty the dishwasher."

"That's sweet. I'm glad you're doing better. Holler if you need anything. I'm on the afternoon trip out, so I need to head to the docks soon. But in the meantime, call me."

"You can count on that. Take care of yourself. Say hi to the whales for me."

Four hours later, miles out in the Atlantic, Olivia stood by Jonathan's side in the wheelhouse aboard the wave cruiser. She felt like Dr. Doolittle's pushmi-pullyu, being yanked in two different directions.

"Beautiful today, isn't it?" Sunlight sparkled off the rippling water.

"Yeah." Jonathan glanced at their heading. "Did Maggie call you this morning?"

"She did. Todd's got her under house arrest until the baby comes." Olivia grinned, then tried to assume a serious expression.

Delighted squeals from the passengers caught Olivia's attention. The massive flukes from a humpback rose above the water, then gracefully dipped below the surface.

Olivia picked up the microphone to describe the whales she loved. Jonathan wordlessly maneuvered the boat for the passengers. She wasn't afraid out here on the water with him. But the thought of his heading out even farther on the sea carved a hole in the pit of her stomach.

Jonathan couldn't get enough of the sea air, the swell of the waves, the freedom of seeing nothing at the horizon. His family and Olivia were what tugged him to shore. They'd held him there since the loss of the *Lady Jane*. That, and his private fear of the past repeating itself. Of course, carpentry helped pay some of the bills, as well.

Today was the last time for a good long while he'd see the whales on a leisurely trip. Terry had already accepted Jonathan's notice. The summer season was drawing to an end, and he wouldn't be needed to pilot anymore. He could hardly wait to set foot on Pete's boat, soon to belong to him via generous financing from a local bank. Somehow, they deemed him a good risk.

Jonathan's light thoughts buoyed him up for the remainder of the afternoon. They docked at last back in the harbor. After performing his final checks on the boat, he headed to the office.

Olivia was standing by Terry's desk when Jonathan entered. Her accusing glare passed from Terry to him.

"Your last day. How come you didn't tell me?"

"I meant to, but I didn't want you to get upset."

"No, I'm not upset. It's just so…soon." Olivia's lips twitched. "You've wanted this for a long time, but wow."

"Sally in the office ordered a cake. It's in the break room," said Terry. "Congratulations, Jon."

Sally, a mother figure to many at the whale watch office, waved a knife. "C'mon, you skinnies, don't be shy. We're proud of our Jon, getting his boat. Chocolate for you, Olivia?"

"Definitely." She gave Jonathan a glance he couldn't quite read. Yes, she was trying to be brave. He could tell from the way she squared her shoulders. But no one could free Olivia from her fear until she was ready.

"Me, too," said Jonathan. "Thanks, everyone. I appreciate the send-off."

"You ever need work, you'll have some here," said Terry.

Olivia stabbed her piece of chocolate cake with a plastic fork. "That, and your carpentry work."

Jonathan nodded. "That's true." He watched her scarf down her cake, then collect her purse from her locker. He set down his plate and followed her to the back door, ignoring the curious looks of the others.

"So, I was hoping we could use that gift card and have dinner before I head out on my first trip," he said as he trailed her to the parking lot.

She stopped at her driver's side door. "That would be nice,

I think. You deserve congratulations. You're…you're very brave, Jonathan Barrotta." She smiled at him, but the grin didn't reach her eyes.

"Thank you." He reached for her hand, which she allowed him to hold. "I have to go, Liv. I can't explain it, but I have to. If I don't, it'll be almost like chickening out."

She nodded. "I know you have to."

"Dinner, Friday night, then?"

"Okay."

The water sprayed over the bow of the *Isabella Rose*. Jonathan, soaked through, stood side-by-side with the crew as they freed the catch and tossed it into the hold. His back and arm muscles screamed from his labors. The skin on his face stung from a salt water rash. And he felt terrific.

All except for his throbbing heart. Had it been just two weeks since he'd watched Olivia drive away? She avoided him at church, and said nothing more to him about the desk she wanted for her father. In fact, she said nothing to him at all.

"It don't get any better than this, does it?" Pete grinned. He measured an undersized fish and tossed it back into the ocean.

Jonathan shook his head. "Nope." He untangled a fine-looking herring and let it fall into the bin with the other fish.

They had been out almost two days, and the entire time Jonathan knew the Lord was confirming His will. This boat would belong to him after he signed the papers at the bank. Some men owned homes. Owning the *Isabella Rose* would be like owning a piece of the sea.

After the catch had been pulled in, the men assembled around the galley table for a hot meal. Stumpy had thrown together a hodgepodge stew for their last night out. Jonathan would be grateful to hold the bowl if but to warm his numb hands.

Pete clomped down from the pilothouse and stopped at the table. "Startin' next month, Jonathan's gonna be your new boss."

Stumpy, a grizzled old fellow, eyed Jonathan. "Huh. Heard you had problems last time out. I'm thinking you're bad luck."

"Listen." Jonathan stood. "I started as a deckhand when I was twelve, working summers. I worked my way up, just like the rest of you. And I know we've all been doing this long enough to know the sea's a fickle lady. All of us have had our share of troubles. But I'm willing to be here no matter what happens."

A few nods and a few suspicious looks. He could mention his faith, but would any of them understand?

Pete must have taken the pause to mean Jonathan was through, so the man continued. "I'm opening my shop in the spring, but in the meantime I'm going to help Jonathan out here in whatever way I can. I expect you to do the same, or you can find work elsewhere."

Stumpy reached over and clapped Jonathan on the back. "If Pete's backin' you, I'm with you, too."

"Yeah, we'll give it a shot." Freddy raised a cup of coffee in toast.

That night, after the men had set out the nets and started to drag them behind the boat, Jonathan collapsed onto his bunk for a few hours' sleep. He touched a snapshot of Olivia tucked into the corner of his bunk. Maggie had given it to him just before they'd shipped out.

Olivia sat on a blanket at the beach, the breeze teasing her hair about her shoulders, her smile lighting her eyes. Maggie had snapped it at the Fourth of July party. Did Olivia remember that night? Jonathan did. It was the night he'd realized he was in love with her.

It was also the night he first mentioned buying the *Isabella Rose* from Pete. He prayed for a way to help Olivia understand somehow that he was meant to be on the sea. Strangely enough, he didn't feel the grip of fear over the past, not even when Stumpy had mentioned what had happened with the *Lady Jane* and Robby. The waves buoyed them along this time. Jonathan imagined the earth and its waters carried safely in

the palm of his Father's hand. With that reminder, he found
his Bible and read a few scriptures, then closed his eyes and
listened to Stumpy snore for the next two hours.

Then Pete bellowed down the hatch for them to come above
deck. The whole routine started again, towing the nets in and
freeing the catch, then storing the fish in the hold.

"Well, that's our quota," Pete said with a sigh.

Jonathan nodded. It was too late in the season to venture farther out, and the two thousand pounds of fish would
hopefully bring a good price back in harbor. The *Isabella
Rose* wouldn't venture out as far as the swordfish boats. Her
crew instead trawled closer to the coast for herring and other
smaller fish in demand by restaurants and markets.

Times had changed since he was a kid working the boats.
The Fisheries Department had assigned quotas for each catch.
Even if they caught more than they could use, they had to toss
back the extra. Plus their fishing days per year were limited.
Bad catch meant less pay. Jonathan echoed Pete's sigh. Next
time, there might not be as many fish.

When they reached the mouth of the harbor, Jonathan
scanned the coastline for the long white building of the Cetacean Institute. Two research vessels were docked at a pier
leading to the entrance of the institute. Was Olivia there? Did
she think of him at all?

He hadn't meant to hurt her. He didn't want her to worry
about him. But then, why did his dream coming true cause
an ache in his heart?

"I've got a project for you, Liv."

Olivia looked up from the microscope and made a nota-
tion of the plankton they'd gleaned from the waters of Stellwagen Bank.

"What kind?"

Rusty, a man with a shock of red hair and crinkles around
his eyes from the sun, glanced at Olivia's notes. "It was Mag-

gie's project, but because she's taken a leave of absence, she recommended you to run with it."

"Okay."

"It's the Whales in Schools program. It's a multimedia program you will share at school assemblies."

"I'll be glad to." Next thing she did would be to call Maggie and thank her.

"Thanks for coming through. Get with Maggie for the particulars. Your first assembly is in less than two weeks."

She studied the printouts and test results before her. In a way, she understood a little of how Jonathan must feel. She'd seen a light in his eyes the night they'd had dinner together and she masked her own trepidation enough to let him enjoy the realization of his dream.

She could envision Jonathan with several days' growth of beard, his dark eyes shining with joy as the wind tousled his wavy hair. The man was born for the water. She prayed for him every night. Olivia dashed away her sullen thoughts, picked up the phone and called Maggie.

"Come over for supper." Maggie sounded jubilant. "I've got scads of notes cluttered around the computer. Plus, I can show you the nursery."

"Wonderful! I'm looking forward to it."

After work she called her dad. "I'm going straight to Maggie's tonight, so eat without me."

"That's fine. I'm starting my computer class at the community college tonight anyway."

She'd forgotten. "Have fun. Don't blow up the hard drive if you can help it." They ended the call laughing. Her dad amazed her, the way he'd picked up computer skills. Every night he checked email and even joined Facebook after she gave him strict warnings about oversharing his personal information and whereabouts online.

If someone wants to find me, Liv, they're going to find me one way or another, he'd said. *The other night, an old friend of mine got back in touch with me. It's fun being on Facebook.*

Olivia left the institute, making a beeline for Todd and Maggie's, enduring the onslaught of Fairport traffic. Her stomach growled. Maybe she should pick up a dessert at the market.

Her heart leaped when she pulled up behind Jonathan's Jeep parked in Maggie's driveway. Olivia pounded on the front door, then opened it when no one answered. "Hello?"

"In the kitchen, Liv!" came Maggie's shout.

The scent of warm tomato sauce and garlic drifted past her. She heard the television in the den blaring sounds from one of the playoff games. If the Red Sox were playing, she knew Jonathan would be glued to his chair. As Olivia tiptoed past the den entrance toward the source of the delightful smells, a quick glance showed Jonathan and Todd entranced by the game.

In one look, Olivia knew she loved Jonathan. The sensation coursed through to her core. Lord help her, she hadn't wanted to fall for someone again. Not like this. The realization made her gasp and quicken her steps to the kitchen when she wanted to flee home.

"Hey." Maggie was bending over an oven rack, poking at a pan of lasagna. "Let me check this and I'll show you my plans for the whale program."

"Hello to you, too. Smells delicious. I should have asked if I needed to bring something." Olivia set her purse on the roomy phone table in the corner. She loved Jonathan, but tonight wasn't the time to think about that.

Maggie closed the oven door. "I'm a lady of leisure now. Utterly domesticated."

"Bet you went kicking and screaming."

"Tell me about it." Maggie rolled her eyes. "I'm doing great, though. Three more months. I have another appointment next week. And Jonathan's starting to build the crib we saw at the store."

Olivia followed Maggie to the little alcove in the kitchen that served as a study. She noted how much Maggie's desk resembled her father's: papers everywhere.

Maggie snatched up a laminated blue folder with a whale decal. "Here it is." She unfolded a series of lessons. "I've designated the program to be for all grade levels. Just pick the presentation you want, from early elementary through high school."

Olivia turned the pages. She could already see herself standing before a classroom of excited students, guiding them through a multimedia presentation about marine life, especially whales. Part of her missed teaching youngsters. "You've put a lot of work into this."

"Yes, it was hard, but thanks to a grant I—well, the institute—received, we were able to fund it, plus a state-of-the-art production company created the program. Which reminds me, I want you to look at another proposal I'm writing." Maggie started riffling through papers on the desk.

"Honestly, Mag, I don't know how you keep it straight."

"I call it organized chaos. Hmm…it's here somewhere." More paper shuffling.

Olivia shook her head. "You should have Jonathan build you a new desk and some file space."

"Not if I'm building one for your dad first."

Jonathan's voice sounded mere inches behind her, and Olivia tried not to startle. Her heart hammered away. She hoped Jonathan couldn't hear it. Olivia turned to face him.

"Hi." Her throat went dry.

"Hey. So, how're things?" His once-sunburned face now had a dark bronze glow.

"Good, good. Work's busy. That's, um, why I'm here tonight mostly. I'm taking care of Maggie's program for the schools until she's back from maternity leave." She liked the cream-colored fisherman knit sweater he wore, which made his hair and eyes seem darker. His mother probably had knitted it and sent it from Florida.

The aroma of burning cheese drifted into the room.

"The lasagna! Ack!" Maggie bounded by them and into

the kitchen. Evidently she broke the stereotype of the pregnant waddle.

"It'll be fine, but you're not supposed to run around like that, remember?" Olivia called around Jonathan's torso. Now she was pinned between him and the desk.

"I'm glad you're here," Jonathan said, obviously ignoring the culinary crisis.

"I—I'm glad you're here, too," Olivia admitted. The scent of his cologne was doing things to her stomach, but it wasn't a bad feeling. She wanted to step a little closer, but also wanted to find something to do in the kitchen away from him.

"Well, you can let me know how big you want me to build your dad's desk."

"Yes. The desk. Of course. We can sketch it out after supper maybe." She tried not to lick her lips. Oh, she'd missed him all right. But he hadn't missed her. He'd only asked about the desk.

"Liv, could you give me a hand with the salad?" Maggie's voice filtered into the alcove.

Olivia ignored Jonathan's probing eyes as she darted around him and joined Maggie in the kitchen.

With rapid strokes of the vegetable peeler, she made quick work of peeling an unwitting cucumber. Then she whacked the thing into slices. Maggie meanwhile pattered back and forth from the table.

"So, what's with the samurai salad technique? You sure it's just veggies you're brutalizing there?" Maggie opened a cabinet to take down some coffee cups.

"I almost made a fool out of myself a minute ago."

"With Jonathan?"

Olivia nodded. "Yeah. It's obvious he's enjoying his new job." She split a head of lettuce in two. "I'm happy for him, really I am."

Maggie's hand closed over the one holding the knife. "You expected him to go out on the water and be miserable?" She gave a soft chuckle. "For men like Jonathan and Todd, it would be like asking them to hate their own souls."

Olivia put down the knife. "No, I don't want him to be miserable. I just—I just want him to miss me." The admission sounded silly when it sprang from her mouth. But her best friend would hear such words and understand.

"I think he does miss you, Liv. You should have seen his face when he came up behind you while we were at the desk. I haven't seen him look so happy in weeks." Maggie sighed.

"But he said he was glad I came, so I could tell him how I wanted Dad's desk built." She'd been fine until she saw Jonathan again. Her emotions now tumbled topsy-turvy inside.

"Men." Maggie rolled her eyes. "He misses you, girl. Believe me."

"I…" Olivia tossed the salad with abandon. "I pray for him, you know."

Maggie smiled. "Then keep praying. Hey, I hear the guys coming. Brace yourself, I think they're hungry."

Chapter 10

Jonathan felt a chill in the air when he first entered Todd's eat-in kitchen, and it wasn't just from the early autumn breeze coming through the window. Olivia kept up a light banter with Maggie, but paid little attention to him. Which was fine with Jonathan, because Todd mentioned wanting to hurry through supper so they could get back to the play-off game.

"So, Liv." Jonathan decided to venture direct conversation with her. "How big do you want your dad's desk to be?"

"You know, I've been thinking about that. Why don't you call him one day, when the two of you are on dry land, and ask him?" Olivia spoke the words evenly and blinked.

"Okay, I'll do that. I'll let you know the cost estimate after I talk to him." He clenched the cup of coffee he held in one hand. *When the two of you are on dry land.* Very funny.

"Great."

Then the conversation changed to the topic of Olivia giving presentations at the schools in the nearby school systems.

What had happened to the sparks between them during the

summer? Maybe the past had needed closure, and that was all. Maybe they had both wanted more than could ever be. He'd felt something tonight when he first saw her by the desk, but then whatever it was left, like air escaping from a tire.

They cleared their plates after supper and Jonathan rejoined Todd in the den for the rest of the game. The score didn't matter to him, or the fact that the Red Sox actually were within a game of winning the sectional title. Olivia waved to them in the den and left, a bundle of materials in her arms.

Jonathan rounded up his courage, stuffed his pride and wiped his sweaty palms on his jeans. "Be right back."

He followed Olivia into the early October night. "Liv."

Olivia laid the bundle of materials on the roof of the car. "Yes?" She turned as she worked the key in the driver's side lock.

"What got your socks in a wrinkle?" He crossed his arms over his chest.

She bit her lower lip. "I—I don't know how to say this." She raised her hands, palms upward, and shrugged. A tentative step brought her closer to him. "I missed you, and you started talking about the desk."

Jonathan closed the gap. "Silly woman, I've missed you. I've missed you, I—" Why were the words so hard to speak? Countless times over the past weeks he'd wanted to tell her somehow.

"I've missed you, too. So much." Olivia blinked rapidly, then gave him a slight smile. "I can't deny you your dream. I can't ask you to give up on what you want so badly. I've tried to trust God to watch out for you, tried not to worry, because I know that bothers you."

"I know you're trying." He allowed himself to cup her cheek with one hand. Her skin was the softest texture he'd touched in a long time.

Olivia's eyes closed, then she touched his hand and pulled it from her cheek. "I think it's best, really, if we remain only friends."

Her statement nailed him like a punch. Jonathan lowered his hand. "You're sure?"

"It's better that way." She swept her fingers across her eyes. "I can't keep putting myself—or you—through this turmoil. I think over time you'd come to resent my fear, and I don't want to hold you back."

"Hold me back?" Jonathan could scarcely draw a breath. "Your fear doesn't hold me back. I'm praying for you, and I know God can handle this."

She nodded. "He can, I'm sure. But I can't. I'm sorry."

Olivia left, not meeting his eyes. Jonathan turned back to the house. Both the conversation and the night air left him numb.

Olivia's high heels made a click-clack on the linoleum as she headed toward the elementary school auditorium. She wore her "power suit," a tailored navy blue skirt and jacket. *Atta girl,* she'd told herself in the mirror. She could do this. The multimedia baggage rolled along behind her. Her first presentation as a representative of CICA, and her stomach was doing somersaults. She imagined a bubbling mass of one hundred third-graders waiting on the edge of their seats.

One of the wheels of the luggage caught on a metal ridge inlaid in the linoleum. She stopped before the cart tipped over.

"Here, let me help you with that," a male voice said, just as Olivia turned and nearly ran into a surprised-looking man wearing a tie.

"Oh, I'm sorry."

He stumbled backward and her own imbalance carried her in his direction. A blur of khaki and white appeared before her eyes. He cushioned their fall to the tile floor. Olivia extricated herself from her awkward position as the man with laughing dark eyes caught his breath. He stood, then reached down to help her up. His hand was strong and warm. "You must be Olivia Shea from the whale institute. I'm Frank Pappalardo."

"Yes, that's me." Her face felt hot as she realized he still held her hand.

Curly ebony hair with dark eyes to match showed Frank's Portuguese ancestry. Somehow he looked familiar to her.

"Ms. Shea, I know this is going to sound bad, but I think I've seen you somewhere before."

"I was going to say the same thing." She felt a run bloom down one leg of her nylons. Great. "Um, I should get to the auditorium to set up." She hoped she wasn't sounding rude.

"I can show you. Another teacher's got my class for a few minutes." Frank took the cart's handle without asking. Olivia slung her purse over one shoulder and grasped her briefcase with her free hand.

"Thanks." She had to stride quickly to keep up with the man's long steps. "Well, you said I looked familiar. Where do you think you've seen me?"

"I've recently started attending Fairport Bible Fellowship, and I think maybe I've seen you there."

So that explained it. "Okay, that's probably why I think I've seen you before, too." She'd noticed him, but then what woman wouldn't?

During the walk through the hallway, Olivia discovered that their fathers probably knew each other, they both liked making homemade pasta and they both were only children. This man piqued her interest, with his open and friendly demeanor. Not to mention an eye-catching smile.

The auditorium doors loomed before them too soon, it seemed. Frank led the way to the platform and helped Olivia, whose fingers turned to all thumbs.

Stop it. Focus. Olivia fumbled with the materials as the roomful of third-graders bounced on their seats and chattered. From the corner of her eye, she saw Frank maneuver his tall frame into an aisle seat.

She missed Jonathan. That was all. The hair and eyes reminded her of him. Had he sailed out again? She steeled herself against the longing that threatened to bubble up. *Remember, you're to stay just friends with the man.*

Frank gave her a smile when he caught her eye, and she fought to keep her focus.

She remembered little of what she said during the following hour, except the children were enthralled. Several volunteers helped her in the presentation. Afterward, the students filed out and Olivia packed her supplies. She wrangled the display materials down the hall and entered the school office to check out. Frank leaned against the counter.

"Hi, again." She smiled and signed out of the school roster.

"I'll see you Sunday morning?" He showed perfect teeth in a perfect mouth on a perfect face.

"Yes, probably." Olivia's mind went blank. "I need to get back to the lab."

She would gladly relinquish this job to Maggie after she returned from maternity leave. Give her the lab work any day. Let Maggie worry about PR.

But then you wouldn't have run into Frank Pappalardo. She paused her mental circle of thoughts. Both she and Jonathan were free. They had come to an impasse. He wouldn't give up his dream of the boat. She wouldn't commit to a man who worked on the ocean. Why, then, did she feel that the idea of entertaining the attentions of another man was almost a betrayal?

Jonathan let the tape measure snap back into its case, then jotted down the figure on his notepad. He could smell the scent of Sam Shea's pipe drifting in from the porch.

"Liv's going to flip when she sees you with that pipe," Jonathan called out the front door.

"That's why I'm finishing now before she gets home from work." Sam coughed, and even inside the front room Jonathan heard the rattle in the man's chest.

"Right. Just like calories vanish if you break a cookie in half, like my mother says." Jonathan joined Sam outside. He paused, but wanted to clear out before Olivia arrived home. He didn't want another replay of their conversation from the other night.

"So you're ganging up on me, too, are ya?"

"Nope." Jonathan chuckled. "You're a grown man. I think your mother finished raising you a long time ago."

Sam blew an *O* of smoke "Now if I can convince my daughter of that, I'll be all set."

"She worries about you." He hadn't meant to chide the man about his habit. And now if he didn't find a quick yet polite way to back out of the conversation, he ran the risk of running into Olivia.

As if Sam sensed Jonathan's thoughts, the older man changed the subject. "She worries about you, too, you know."

"Yeah."

"And I know you can't help it."

"What do you mean?"

Sam shifted on the rocking chair. "First time you went back out, I think she relived several years ago, when she said good-bye to someone else she loved."

Loved? She loved him? Jonathan's head swam. Of course Olivia had been irritated the other night, the way he'd talked about the desk. But then she said they should remain only friends. *Women.*

"There she is now." Sam gave a nod as Olivia's car pulled into the driveway.

"Guess I should go." From his spot on the porch, Jonathan saw the dismay on Olivia's face.

"Stay for supper." Sam coughed. "Don't know what's on for tonight. Friday's pretty low-key around here." His rough hand slid the now-extinguished pipe into his pocket.

The car door slammed, then Olivia headed toward the porch. "Hey, Dad, Jonathan." She looked as happy to see him as someone going for a root canal.

"Jon's staying for supper tonight. I figured he and I can

hash over the details for the desk." Sam and Jonathan followed Olivia into the house.

"Now, Sam, I don't have to..." Jonathan began.

"That's fine if you stay, Jonathan." Olivia was staring at the floor. "I, uh, have plans tonight, so I won't be here for dinner."

"Is that so?" Sam's eyebrows shot up. "Hmm, suppose me and Jonathan could go to the Sea Dawg for a bite, us two bachelors."

Yes, that sounded fine to Jonathan, too. Usually forthcoming about her activities, Olivia had clamped her lips together after mentioning her plans, which probably meant one thing: She had a date. And Jonathan didn't want to be here when the guy arrived.

Olivia didn't watch Jonathan's Jeep pull away outside. Frank would meet her at the Sea Dawg in less than an hour, and here she was, still in her work clothes. She hurried through a shower and into a comfortable dress. But they were only having dinner at the best greasy spoon in town.

The whine of the hair dryer masked Olivia's sigh. She couldn't stop thinking about Jonathan. He was a good friend, and she wanted to keep him as a friend, even if she had to release her love for him.

If she could distance herself enough from Jonathan, perhaps in time the ache would go away.

"You look frightful," she said to the reflection with brown wavy hair gently cascading to its shoulders. "Anyone would think you were getting ready for a funeral by the expression on your face."

Olivia tried to brighten her thoughts. Frank had mentioned grabbing a snack, then going to the high school's one-act play night. Frank had called nearly every night for the past week, and she felt comfortable getting to know him.

Lord, my life is getting on track again. I'm doing the work I love, still here with Dad because he needs me. And now someone like Frank's come along. He's a nice guy.... Olivia applied some eyeliner. She needed to forget her feelings for Jonathan. There was no way out of their stalemate that she could see. A friendly night out with Frank would be a good way to begin to put Jonathan out of her heart.

"Now, would you look at that?" Sam nodded toward the doorway of the Sea Dawg.

Jonathan took a sip of coffee before turning around in his chair, and he almost choked.

A tall man with dark curly hair was helping Olivia with her coat. Her hair hung loose and glowed a golden brown under the lighting. Her emerald green dress hugged her curves demurely and revealed a flash of knee. Jonathan faced back around before Olivia saw him staring.

"I knew she'd met the new teacher at the elementary school, but I had no idea it was Nazarro Pappalardo's boy." Sam continued to look across the room, his blue eyes undoubtedly watching his daughter and her date.

"Didn't the Pappalardos move away years ago? I remember that name from grade school." From the corner of his eye, Jonathan saw them escorted to one of the window tables. Like a gentleman, Frank seated Olivia before seating himself. They opened the laminated menus.

"Yeah. Nazarro's brother Isadore still lives here. I just saw him yesterday, and he mentioned Frank was in town again. A shame that boy broke family tradition and got a land job." Sam shook his head.

"It happens." Jonathan flipped the bill over and reached for his wallet.

"You going to get a refill of coffee and try not to stare at Liv and Frank?"

"I'd rather not. I need to get some prices for boat parts. Pete's signed the boat over to me and it needs a good overhaul before I go out again."

The two men paid the bill and left the restaurant. Olivia

had given no sign that she'd seen either her father or Jonathan, for which Jonathan was grateful.

"You sure you haven't bitten off more than you can chew, son?" Sam asked as they walked to the Jeep.

Jonathan shook his head. "No, I knew what I was getting into." He didn't bother to say the past two runs had been dismal, and he'd started dipping into his reserve funds for expenses.

"Why don't you come on in?" Sam unlocked the front door of the house. "I can show you the boat suppliers' sites on the internet. You can even print out a price list." Sam paused, then coughed. "Oughta put some of my learning from that computer class to use."

"Sure, why not?"

When they entered the house, Jonathan could smell a whiff of Olivia's perfume lingering in the air. Sam cracked his knuckles, pushed a button and the computer whirred to life. Within a few minutes Sam had pulled up some websites for boat engines.

"This is great, Sam. I need to write these down."

"Never mind that. Watch." He pushed a button, and the price list printed. A coughing fit racked his body. Sam snatched a tissue from the box on the desk and held it to his mouth.

"Hey, are you okay?"

Sam nodded and mumbled around the tissue. "This will pass. Just a fall bug I picked up. Do me a favor. Make a pot of decaf, would you?"

"Sure." Jonathan left for the kitchen. Something was wrong with Sam. He felt it in his gut. He got the coffee brewing, all the while thinking of ways to convince the man he needed to see a doctor. More coughing came from the front room.

Maybe someone could talk some sense into the mule-headed lobsterman. Jonathan squared his shoulders, preparing to announce that coffee would be ready soon. He froze when he saw Sam sitting at the desk.

He hadn't seen so much blood in one place since Stumpy bashed his head on his bunk the last time they'd shipped out. The tissue Sam held up to his mouth bloomed red, and drops of blood had spattered on his shirt and onto the hardwood floor.

Chapter 11

"Thanks. I had fun." Olivia shivered in the chilly air as Frank escorted her to her front door. She appreciated his following her home to make sure she arrived all right.

"I did, too. It was nice seeing the town again, even if we missed the play." Frank's eyes glowed under the porch light. They'd gone for a drive in his car, past the high school stomping grounds and to the harbor park.

"I can make us some more coffee if you want to stay for a bit. Dad might be up." She noted her father's truck in the driveway and wondered about his reaction to Frank.

"Sounds good."

Olivia's key turned too easily in the lock, and when she turned to push the door open, she expected to see the glow of lights from the living room and hear the late news show blaring. Pop would be snoring in the easy chair.

Then she saw the bloody tissues on the floor in front of the desk.

"What in the world?" Her pulse leaped into her throat.

Frank stood next to her in the front room. "What's wrong?"

"I need to find out what happened to Dad." She gestured to the tissues. Her stomach had tied itself into a knot. "Dad? Where are you?" She checked her phone, which she'd muted. Jonathan had called an hour ago.

Lights were on throughout the downstairs and a full pot of coffee waited on the kitchen counter. The linen closet door was open, and a few towels had fallen to the floor. As Olivia scanned the empty house, pinpricks of dread tingled her spine.

"I need to call Jonathan." Olivia noticed the answering machine light blinking.

She played the message. "Liv, it's Jon. I brought your dad to the E.R. tonight. He's got pneumonia, so they want to keep him." The phone line crackled. "If you get home before midnight, come to the E.R.—they don't expect to have a room for him by then. I'll wait for you."

Olivia felt chilled to the core at Jonathan's words, but hearing his voice sent a warmth through her that dulled the cold. Frank's hand held her elbow.

"I'll drive you."

"Thanks. I need to get some things for Dad in case they keep him." *Think, don't panic, think.*

She pounded up the stairs to her father's room. Olivia couldn't remember the last time she'd entered the hallowed territory.

The picture of a dark-haired woman wearing a prim sweater and a pearl necklace smiled at Olivia. She ignored the impulse to turn the picture of her mother facedown on the nightstand. Instead, Olivia found one of her dad's work shirts, some underclothes, pajamas and a pair of pants in the bureau.

He'd kept her mother's picture. Her mother still smiled at Olivia's dad each night before he turned in. Was that why he sometimes fell asleep downstairs at night? Why didn't he just put her photo away for good?

"And if he got rid of your picture, you'd be gone forever."

Olivia shivered and rubbed her arms. She'd have to turn on the heat before she left.

No time now, though, to let any feelings about her mother resurface. Frank waited downstairs and Dad needed her. Olivia prayed for strength to make it through the next hours with her emotions intact. The fact that Jonathan and Frank would both be with her seemed unimportant. She'd deal with any awkward moments if or when they happened.

Jonathan drank the last sip of his third cup of coffee from the vending machine. He was running out of change and his body screamed for sleep. He'd come in that morning, early, from a fishing trip and hadn't rested. Now he wished he had.

His second wind came when he saw Olivia enter the emergency room's sliding doors. She carried an overnight bag and her gaze met his. Frank Pappalardo followed in her wake.

"Where's Dad?" Olivia placed the overnight bag on the floor.

Then she was in Jonathan's arms, holding on as if he were a lifeline. Jonathan allowed himself to breathe in the scent of her hair, still down around her shoulders. She trembled as he held her.

Remembering Frank, Jonathan released her from the hug, but kept an arm around her shoulders and took the bag. "He's still in an exam room. They've given him an antibiotic shot and some breathing treatments to clear up his lungs, and he's on oxygen now."

"I want to talk to his nurse or doctor or whoever's in charge." She looked around the room as though she would pounce on the next official-looking person wearing scrubs who came in her direction.

"We'll find someone. There's the nurse who gave him the shot. We'll talk to her." Jonathan steered Olivia toward the clerk writing notes on a clipboard. He noticed Frank had taken a seat.

Jonathan introduced Olivia to the nurse, who escorted her back to the exam room wing of the E.R.

Frank had removed his tie when Jonathan returned to the waiting area. Even though Frank looked tired, he still wore the *GQ* look women went nuts over. Jonathan couldn't remember the last time he had worn a tie. He wasn't quite sure if he owned one.

"Hey, I'm Jonathan Barrotta." He extended his hand, which Frank shook. Jonathan took the seat across from Frank.

"Frank Pappalardo."

"Yeah. You used to live here when we were kids. Sam told me earlier."

Frank nodded. "I came back to work and be near some of my family. I never liked living in the mountains in western Mass. Too landlocked for me."

Jonathan had seen Frank in church but hadn't introduced himself yet. It didn't seem they had much in common. Except for the Lord and Olivia. There had to be something else to talk about, to break the ice. Jonathan didn't want to clam up and act like a jerk, even if Frank had spent more time with Olivia tonight than Jonathan had in the last month.

"So, you been following the playoffs?" Jonathan ventured with a question.

Frank nodded. "In fact, my uncle's hoping to get World Series tickets if the Sox make it. Wouldn't that be something?" Then he laughed. "Imagine that. Maybe they'd win."

Jonathan snorted. "Yeah! That'd be something, all right, considering the Pats' Super Bowl win."

Conversation fell flat after that. A schoolteacher, that's what Frank did for a living. What would he and a fisherman have to talk about? Jonathan secretly hoped Frank would leave.

"You teach school?"

"Yeah, third grade. I've got my hands full, but I love kids. I like knowing I'm having an impact on their future." Frank's face took on an animated expression as he began telling stories of "his kids," as he called them. In a way, Jonathan realized, the man reminded him of Robby. He had the same charisma, open smile and charming nature. And it took a special man to devote his career to children. Of course Olivia liked Frank.

An hour later, Olivia appeared. She hesitated as though not sure about which man to sit near, then settled onto a chair a few seats down from both of them.

"Well, Dad's doing okay. He's in his room now. They, uh, found a spot on his right lung so they're going to do a CAT scan in the morning." She looked from Frank to Jonathan. "Thanks, guys, for staying so late. I appreciate it." A pretty blush suffused her cheeks.

Frank spoke up first. "It's no problem. Are you ready to go now, or are you staying longer?"

She grinned. "Dad ordered me to go home and rest. I can come back in the morning."

Jonathan stood. She came with Frank, and she'd leave with Frank. He could live with that. He knew when to back off when she and Robby started dating. He could do the same again.

"Good night, then. Liv, if there's anything I can do…" The words sounded feeble to his ears.

"Thanks, Jon. You've been terrific. I'm glad you were there tonight." Her voice caught. She squeezed his arm.

But as he left, Jonathan knew she wouldn't call him. Not as long as she had Frank around.

The house had warmed up nicely by the time Olivia arrived home. Frank walked her to the door, and they said good-night, which was nearly all they'd said since leaving the hospital. She wanted to talk to someone and his friendship felt too new to lay this on him. Poor Frank.

Olivia showered again, letting the water warm her chilled soul and turn her fingers wrinkly. Once settled into her warm terry cloth robe and slippers, she sat at the kitchen table with a cup of decaf coffee and her Bible. No matter that it was after one in the morning. Sleep could wait.

Oh, Dad, why didn't you listen? Why didn't you get rid of that tobacco years ago? She wouldn't allow herself to think the worst. Maybe the doctors had made a mistake about the spot on his lung. Tomorrow morning when she went to the hospital, she would find her dad driving the nurses nuts and packing to go home. He would resume griping about the high price of diesel fuel and mumbling that the market lobster prices needed to be higher.

Olivia started to pray, then fumbled over her words. "Why, God? Why now?" she muttered at the sacred pages before her. "It's always like playing Russian roulette when I pray. I prayed—" Her voice caught in her throat.

The image came back to her of a little girl with brown pigtails, hands folded as she knelt at her bedside, begging God for her mommy to come home to them. No answer. Then Robby. A resounding "no." More recently, Maggie and the baby. She got her answer that time. Both were still safe and doing well. And now, Olivia poised at the edge of asking God to help again.

"I'm sorry, Lord. I'm afraid to ask You. Afraid I'll be disappointed again." She whisked a fallen tear from the thin page. "I don't know what to do."

After several minutes of listening to the furnace powering up to cycle heat through the house, listening to the coffeepot gurgle on the counter and the refrigerator compressor cycle on, Olivia stood up and sighed. The heavens were as brass. Her well-ordered life was a sham. Under the still waters, the current churned violently. She spent a restless night, dreading the coming morning.

Jonathan whistled under his breath as he walked to Sam's hospital room. After a few cups of coffee, he actually felt half-human. Maybe Olivia would be with her father. He wasn't sure whether he hoped to see her or not.

He knocked softly on the door frame before entering. Sam was dabbing at a plate of fruit, yogurt and toast while the television blared news from the twenty-four-hour station.

"Hey, Sam. You scared us last night."

"I still say I've got one of those autumn colds." Sam swallowed, then continued. "They already sent me down for a scan. The doctor's going to let me know soon when I can go home."

"Uh-huh." Jonathan settled into the soft vinyl-covered chair by the window. He peeked out through the blinds. "It's a great day out. I'm pulling out again come Monday. I hope the weather holds."

"It should." Sam struck his fist on the bed table. "I've gotta check my traps. I need to bring them in, get to the market. Aye, there's always something. Do you think they'd notice if I slipped out the back door?"

"Yes, sir. It would be pretty quiet around here."

"Watch it, son." Sam's eyes twinkled despite his gruff tone.

"What would be quiet around here?" Olivia said as she came into the room. "Have you been hassling the nurses, Dad?"

"Just when they won't let me go to the bathroom without permission. At least they let me change into my own pajamas." Sam huffed and sipped his coffee.

Olivia laughed as she stood by her father's bed, but Jonathan noticed dark circles under her eyes. "Please, go easy on them."

"And you, missie." He rubbed Olivia's arm. "You quit losing sleep over me. I've got lots of lobsters to trap, a boat to work on. I'm not going anywhere."

"I'll try not to worry."

"Barrotta, you keep an eye on her for me."

"Now, Sam, I don't think Liv needs watching over."

"Are you arguing with me?"

Olivia spoke up. "Dad, I'll be fine. In fact, Frank called this morning and his uncle Isadore has offered to haul your pots in for you and take everything to market. So you concentrate on getting better."

"Good morning, Mr. Shea." A young man in a white lab coat and a stethoscope dangling around his neck stood in the doorway. "I'm Dr. Misek. Dr. McKinley's at a conference this week, but we've notified his office that you've been admitted. So, how are you feeling this morning?"

Sam shifted higher on the bed. "Doing great. I'm ready to go home."

Dr. Misek nodded. "Good, good. I'm going to have some more labs drawn this morning and check your breathing, and if all goes well you'll go home this afternoon. First, though, I've got the results of your scan."

Jonathan joined Olivia at her father's bedside. Her fingers clamped around the bed rail. He wanted to rest a hand on her shoulder, to assure her he was there.

"The mass in your right lung is about two centimeters long by one centimeter wide. It's too early to tell right now if it's cancerous. We'll cross that bridge after we get the infection in your body under control and can schedule a biopsy." His gentle tones made Olivia relax her hold on the bed rail. Jonathan wondered if her fingers had made indentations in the metal. "But I want to schedule that biopsy as soon as possible. After that, we'll know what we're dealing with."

"All right, Doc. If there's something in my lung that doesn't belong, I want it out. Thanks for giving it to me straight." Sam sighed, and Olivia frowned. He glanced up at her. "Now, Liv, don't look like that. I'm going to fight this, whatever it is."

Chapter 12

Late October came to the North Shore, and with it the exhilaration of a New England fall. Olivia left the institute after a long afternoon of lectures for undergraduates and lab work, her brain still reeling from her independent study course on the migration of cetaceans.

If she hadn't taken Terry's offer of a job this past summer, she wouldn't have been here for Dad. Olivia offered a prayer of thanks as she drove home, anticipating a supper of homemade pasta with her father and Frank.

Three weeks ago her father had come home from the hospital. After a nail-biting biopsy that confirmed a cancerous growth, her father had started radiation treatments to help shrink the growth before surgery.

Then there was tomorrow. By this time tomorrow, her father would be recovering from surgery, having part of his lung removed. The most stubborn man she had ever known would soon be dependent on her for many things, at least for a while.

A familiar Jeep zoomed by in the Fairport traffic. There

went the second most stubborn man Olivia had ever known. She hadn't spoken to Jonathan since the morning in the hospital when they'd found out the CAT scan results. Several times, she'd looked at his number on her phone, then stopped short of pushing the button. What was there to say?

Olivia pulled into the driveway and noticed her father had company. Frances O'Leary stood on the porch, facing the front door and shifting her weight from one foot to the other.

Olivia gathered her briefcase and tote bag, and met the woman on the porch. "Hi, Mrs. O'Leary." Her throat had sawdust in it as she recalled their last meeting, the ugly confrontation in the grocery store last summer.

"I'm stopping by to let you and your father know that the Fishermen's Wives Auxiliary plans to drop off meals over the next two weeks while your father recovers from surgery." Frances's mouth had deeper lines around it than Olivia remembered.

"Thanks, Frances. Um, would you like to come in for some coffee or something? I'm going to be starting supper soon, but I think Dad will be happy to have a visitor."

As Olivia expected, a look of surprise crossed Frances's face. "I'm afraid I can't stay today, but when I bring my meal for you, I'll stay a while. We'll—we'll be praying for your dad tomorrow." With that, Frances shouldered her purse and left for her car.

Olivia's dad was checking his email when she entered the front room. "How's it going, Dad?" She planted a kiss on his head.

"I'm hungry. I want to hurry up and eat before seven since I can't eat later. So, hop to it." He clicked on the mouse.

"You got it." Olivia kicked her shoes off and set her briefcase on the floor next to the desk. "By the way, Frances O'Leary was outside. She said the Fishermen's Wives Auxiliary is making some meals for us after you get home from the hospital."

"Isn't that nice of them? I sure hope Frances doesn't make her prize meat loaf. Tastes like compressed cardboard."

Olivia laughed as she walked to the kitchen. "When did you have her meat loaf?"

"Oh, before you came along your mother and I used to visit with the O'Learys quite a bit. Nice couple."

"Ah." Olivia concentrated on measuring the flour for her homemade pasta. "Frank should be here soon. He had a meeting after school, but he promised to come straight over."

"Good, good. He's a nice young man. As steady as they come. I'm glad you've got a new friend."

Olivia let the subject of her relationship with Frank alone. But she had to agree she was glad for his friendship. He would pray with her, listen to her and make her laugh at his adventures in the classroom. And hopefully, she was good for him, too.

Frank arrived just as Olivia had put the Alfredo sauce mixture on the stove to reheat. He brought a bouquet of wildflowers for the table and a jug of homemade apple cider.

"It'll be just the thing on a cold night like tonight," Frank said. "I brought some paperwork for school to catch up on. Hope you don't mind."

"Not at all. I've got some ideas to organize for my dissertation." But Olivia had planned on keeping herself busy tomorrow at the hospital with her paperwork.

A knock sounded at the front door just before the three of them sat down to supper.

"Now, I wonder who that could be?" Her father's tone made Olivia's suspicions rise.

Her father ambled to the front room while Olivia and Frank waited. The door creaked open.

"Well, hello there, Jon!" her father boomed. "C'mon in! We're just sitting down to supper. Oh? You and Todd can set the desk in the front room." The storm door smacked closed. Then came the sounds of struggling and something large being toted inside.

"Oh, it must be Dad's desk," Olivia explained to Frank. "Jonathan built it. I'm sure Dad's thrilled it's finished before he goes in for surgery." *And I just bet he's thrilled at tonight's timing.*

"Jonathan seems to be one talented man."

"Yes, he is. Would you like some salad?" Olivia passed the bowl to Frank. Their fingers brushed and heat rushed to her face without her expecting it. If she knew her dad at all, he'd invite Jonathan to supper.

If Olivia had invited him for supper instead of Sam, Jonathan would have said no. He would have assumed Olivia was inviting him because she had to. Sam did because he wanted to.

He followed Sam—and Frank's cologne trail—to the dining room, where Olivia sat, blushing, across from Frank. She leaped to her feet and darted to the kitchen cabinets and returned with another plate and a place setting for him.

"Thanks, Liv."

"You're welcome." She passed him the bowl of steaming pasta. "So, how's the fishing been?"

"It could be better. The past two runs barely covered expenses. One of the guys might call it quits for the season." He hadn't wanted to talk about his problems tonight.

Frank spoke up. "Can you get a replacement?"

"Probably." Was this guy here every night after school, a stack of papers under his arm?

Shame rushed over Jonathan at his uncharitable thoughts. Frank was a Christian brother. But from the glances Frank gave Olivia across the table during the meal, Jonathan guessed Frank wanted to be more than brotherly to Olivia.

If Olivia wanted a man with a safe, stable occupation, Frank was ideal for her. The other three at the table laughed at a joke Frank told, that a student had told him. Jonathan smiled, not wanting to show he'd missed the punch line because he'd zoned out.

After supper, Sam and Jonathan moved the contents from Sam's old desk to the new one. Olivia was heating up some apple cider in the kitchen, and the sweet smell made Jonathan's mouth water.

"Hope this works." Frank turned on Sam's computer. "All right, you're back in business, Sam."

"Here, guys." Olivia stood in the archway that separated the front room from the living room. She held a tray with four mugs of steaming cider. "I put cinnamon sticks in, so take 'em out if you don't like them."

"Thanks." Jonathan helped himself to a mug.

Sam hunched over the new desk and initiated the internet connection. "Jon, let me show you this engine website I found. I might have found the schematics for that engine that's been troubling you."

"Liv," Frank said as he held open the front door, "c'mon outside. We'll enjoy the fall air."

Jonathan didn't bother to look at her when she passed the new desk. He looked at the technical drawing instead. "Can you print that out for me, please?"

Sam hit the button. "Here it comes."

"Are you ready for tomorrow?" he asked Sam. The door clicked behind Olivia and Jonathan breathed easier.

"As ready as a body can be." Sam sighed and stood upright. "Figure I'm getting what I deserve."

"Why would you think that?"

"Liv's nagged at me for years to quit the smoking, and I didn't listen." Sam blinked at the computer screen. "I'm being punished. And I'm scared."

Jonathan prayed for the right words. "God loves you, Sam. He wants the best for you. I know He disciplines his children, what dad doesn't sometimes? But that you're being punished, how can you say that for sure?"

Another ragged breath from Sam, followed by a cough. "I don't know…"

"Okay, what if you kept every lobster you trapped, even

the small ones, then what would happen to the lobster population?"

"Well, it would go down."

"It doesn't mean lobsters are meant to die out and become extinct?"

"Course not. Trapping and keeping undersized lobsters would make the population go down. It's a natural effect." Jonathan saw realization dawn in Sam's eyes.

"Then what's happening to you now is probably a natural effect of your habit."

Sam nodded. "The radiation shrunk the tumor, did I tell you?"

"No. God's watching out for you." Emboldened, Jonathan continued. "Could I pray with you about the surgery tomorrow?" Jonathan's throat swelled at the thought of anything happening to this dear man who'd become like a second father to him.

"I'd like that."

They bowed their heads.

Olivia heard the murmuring voices inside the house. Outside in the chilly air, part of her wanted to remain indoors. But Frank's idea was a good one. She shivered involuntarily.

A warmth settled around her shoulders, and Frank's hand brushed her hair. "Is that better?"

"Er, I'm fine, thanks." She sipped her cider, feeling like an adolescent. Was this really what she wanted? "Sorry, I just need to walk around a little. I feel fidgety tonight."

The last night she'd been on the porch with someone, she'd been with Jonathan. Olivia remembered sharing part of her heart and part of her fear with him. Her lips tingled with the memory of the almost-kiss.

How had she ended up on the porch with someone else, then? It had been her choice, she reminded herself. The last day Jonathan had piloted for the whale-watching tours, Olivia had resigned herself to letting him go.

"I'll make sure Uncle Isadore keeps up with your dad's lobster pots." Frank interrupted her pondering and pacing the porch.

"Thanks. It helps to know that Dad and I have such good friends." She turned and faced Frank, who had settled onto the porch swing.

He set his mug on the little table and joined her at the porch railing. "You're a special woman, Olivia Shea. A man would be a fool not to recognize that."

She couldn't breathe. She shouldn't have come out on the porch with him. He was too close....

The front door opened and the porch light came on. Olivia blinked. Her face suffused with heat, she turned to focus on Jonathan who had said something to her father inside.

Then his eyes met hers. "Good night, Liv. I'll stop by the hospital to see Sam before I ship out again. G'night, Frank."

He walked to his Jeep without a backward glance and sped off into the night.

"Maggie, I'm glad you're here." Olivia shivered in the hospital hallway. She despised the antiseptic smell that turned her stomach. "I know Todd watches over you like a hawk, and I'm honored he's let you be here while Dad's in surgery."

Maggie looked like she'd hidden a beach ball under her oversized sweater. She smiled and rubbed her stomach. "What better place for an extremely gravid woman like myself to be?"

They linked arms and continued to the chapel. Olivia allowed herself a chuckle, a sound that seemed rather frivolous lately. "I can always count on you to make me laugh."

She pushed through the wooden door and into the serene chapel, dimly lit and smelling of fresh lemon furniture polish. A dark-haired woman was sitting in the front row, her head bowed reverently.

Olivia settled onto the nearest bench and made room for Maggie. "This is such a peaceful place. A storm could be going on outside and you'd never know."

"Yes, I could fall asleep here quite easily." Maggie yawned.

"So, how are you feeling? You look, as you put it, quite gravid. I should have come by more often, instead of just to talk about work."

"Hey, the whales program has taken off. I've been getting nothing but rave reviews by email. And it's thanks to you." Maggie bit her lip as though she wanted to say more.

"It was your project. I'm just following your directions. Speaking of which, pray for me. I'm going out with Rusty on his tagging program. We're combining our efforts for our theses. He's going to tag some of the whales and track their migration. For my help, I'm getting access to his data." Olivia lowered her voice further when the lady in the front row cast a quick glance to where they sat. "Anyway, with Dad recovering from surgery and all, I don't know how to fit it all in. And I won't leave Dad longer than I have to."

"Don't worry. If you've got to go out—and I know you do—I'll hang out with your dad."

"Are you sure? He's pretty crusty but doesn't bite."

"I know." Maggie grinned. Then she gasped and touched her stomach. "Ouch. That was quite a kick, sweetie. I don't mind being housebound for you, not one bit."

Olivia marveled at the tiny ripple that crossed Maggie's abdomen. "Oh, she's strong. May I?" She reached out.

"Of course."

Beneath her fingers resting on the woven cotton sweater, Olivia felt the surge of life. "Maggie…it's so amazing…. I've read Psalm 139 many times, but this…this makes it real."

"Someday it'll be your turn."

"I hope so. I really do."

"I'm praying that you and Jonathan somehow work things out."

Olivia removed her hand from Maggie's stomach and sat up straighter. "Thanks, I think. Right now, though, I'm working at forgetting how I feel." She studied a felt banner on the wall.

"Don't let your fear make you miss out on the love of a lifetime." Maggie's eyes challenged her. "Plus, what's this about you and that teacher?"

"Frank Pappalardo. We're friends. He goes to our church, you know."

"He's a nice guy. Todd and I met him last week. He said he knew you, that you'd been spending time together. Betcha he keeps both feet on dry ground."

"What's that supposed to mean? A relationship with Frank would be safe because he's not a fisherman?"

"I didn't say that."

Olivia looked at the altar aglow with soft electric candle-light. "He's a good Christian man. Plus we have a good time together."

"Well, I guess I'm glad for you, then."

"Liar."

"I hate it when we disagree."

"We'll have to agree to disagree, then." Olivia grinned.

Maggie snorted. "I'll just have to pray some more." She shifted to her feet. "Okay, I've got the fidgets, dear. I'll do a couple of laps around the hallway and come back." She shifted to her feet and waddled from the room.

Chapter 13

She hadn't meant to start a spat with Maggie. Or disturb the woman who'd been praying at the front of the chapel. The lady stood, reached for her purse and smiled at Olivia. Her designer suit made a soft swish as she headed down the aisle for the door. There was something about her—

When the woman paused as she passed Olivia's bench, Olivia cleared her throat. "Excuse me. I'm sorry if my friend and I disturbed your prayers. My dad's in surgery today and we wanted a peaceful place to sit."

"I barely heard you. You weren't a bother at all." Her dark hair was swept up in an elegant French twist, her makeup skillfully applied, making her age a number Olivia couldn't guess. Despite her smile, the woman's dark brown eyes held a deep sadness.

"So," Olivia continued, "are you waiting on a family member?"

"My—my husband." The woman spoke the words as if they were foreign to her. "He's having surgery. It's cancer."

Olivia's heart pounded in her ears. She assessed the woman's face, her mind's eye whisking her back to her living room, to the mantel where a picture from long ago still sat covered in dust. *It can't be...*

The woman's eyes filled with tears. "You're...Olivia."

"You're..." Olivia couldn't speak the word.

The woman gave a slow nod. "Belinda Reilly Shea, except I haven't gone by Shea for a long time."

Olivia's head reeled. Should she hug this woman standing before her? Scream at her? Slap her? Or run from the room? She stood, now eye-to-eye with the woman who'd borne her and disappeared one day.

She shook the hand offered her, noting manicured nails and elegant fingers. Olivia looked at her own hands, with similar fingers although nails cut short.

"How did you know about Dad?"

"We, uh, we got back in touch on Facebook not too long ago. He called me and told me about his diagnosis the other day. So I knew I had to come. It's long past time." She hung her head low.

A flood of questions crashed from one end of Olivia's head to the other. Riding on the crest of the flood was the white-hot anger she thought she'd buried for good.

"So, you come now. Is that supposed to make up for the past twenty-some years?" A pent-up torrent threatened to pour from Olivia's mouth. She clamped her lips closed before the tirade commenced. *God, help me. Please.*

"No," her mother whispered. "I can never atone for the lost years. I know I don't deserve to be called your mother."

Just like the prodigal son. The thought came, unbidden. He had no claim to anything of his family's, but went home for better or worse. Olivia gritted her teeth. Would Christ welcome her mother home?

But, Lord, You don't understand. She's betrayed me.

I was betrayed, too.

She realized she stood silently while Belinda eyed her,

from hair to toes. Olivia managed to say, "I don't know how much longer they'll be, but…I could use a cup of coffee. How about it?"

Belinda smiled, the same wry grin Olivia had seen reflected in her mirror for as long as she could remember. "I'd like that."

They left the chapel. Olivia felt like a dentist had given her shots of anesthetic all over, as if she moved in some surreal dream that had turned into a nightmare. *Jonathan, I need you.*

Jonathan waited in his Jeep, debating whether he should go inside the hospital. He knew Maggie was there, waiting by Olivia's side. He wanted to be there, too.

He rested his head on the steering wheel. "Lord, I don't know what to do. You know I love Olivia with all that's in me. But I don't know how to approach her. I don't want the past to always loom between us.

"And this Frank. I won't stand in their way. Give me the wisdom to handle this relationship with Olivia. I don't know what to say to her sometimes."

He exited the Jeep and crossed the parking lot. After he found out how Sam's surgery went, he would ship out, long enough for the cold water of the North Atlantic to numb his heart.

The sliding doors whooshed open to let him through, and Jonathan followed the signs to the surgery wing of the hospital. Maggie was sipping from a bottle of spring water in the waiting room.

"Hey!" She shifted to stand.

"Don't get up." He took a seat next to her. "Have you heard anything yet?"

Maggie shook her head. "Not yet. I hate it when these things take so long. I left Liv in the chapel."

"How's she doing?"

"Quite well, all things considered." Maggie paused as if she wanted to say more. "I think she'll be glad you're here."

"I hope so." Jonathan watched a couple across the room, their weathered and wrinkled fingers entwined. Years of trust mirrored in each other's gaze.

"Um, if it's any consolation, I don't think she and Frank are really dating." Maggie sighed.

"Ah," was Jonathan's response. He didn't want to mention walking out on the porch that one night, seeing Frank with Olivia. Their relationship might not be serious now, but it could very well head that way. A gurgling sound made Jonathan glance around.

"Oh. My stomach." Maggie laughed. "Have you had lunch yet?"

"No."

"Well, come to the cafeteria with me and we'll grab something."

They walked the halls slowly to the elevator, then went to the cafeteria floor. Across the crowded room, he saw Olivia and another woman having coffee.

Jonathan and Maggie bought sandwiches and drinks, then Jonathan carried their tray over to Olivia's table. The look on Olivia's face and the expression in her brown eyes wrenched Jonathan's gut. What was wrong? Had something happened to Sam?

"Hi, there. Mind if we join you two?" Maggie pulled one of the extra chairs out and settled into it. "Aah, that's better. I'm afraid I don't know you. I'm Maggie Donovan." Jonathan set their tray on the table and boldly took the vacant seat next to Olivia.

"Hi, Maggie. I'm Belinda." The women shook hands, and Jonathan introduced himself, as well.

Belinda explained that she was waiting for her husband, who was having surgery, and that she and Olivia had met in the chapel. Olivia sipped her coffee and said nothing as Belinda talked about her flourishing real estate business west of Boston. She was in Fairport for the week.

"So, Jonathan, you're a fisherman." Belinda's dark eyes flashed a glance to Olivia, then back to him.

"Yes, I am. I work a trawler, taking in herring and other kinds of market fish. I'm leaving Monday morning for another run." He started on his sandwich. Maybe they shouldn't take too long at lunch. Olivia had the look of a cornered animal. He would hurry through his meal, especially if his presence bothered her.

"That's a dangerous job." A worry line appeared on Belinda's forehead.

He nodded. "It is, but if you keep your eyes open and follow your instincts—plus the weather reports—you can keep safe and make money, too." His right hand still had stitches from when a fish's spiny fins had torn through his weathered gloves and into his palm.

"I guess it takes a special kind of man to do a job like that." Belinda sipped her coffee.

"Er, I don't know about that. But it's not for everybody. I know I couldn't sell houses." Jonathan turned his hand over and glanced at his palm. Too late he saw Olivia follow his glance.

"Jonathan—" Olivia reached for his hand "—when did this happen?" Her fingers gently traced the stitches on his palm, sending ripples of electricity down the nerve endings of his spine. Forgetting this woman would be a miracle.

"Last week. It's healing up fine." Jonathan didn't bother to tell her that underneath the first layer of stitches was another, deeper layer that secured the tendons together. He decided to downplay his injury.

"Please be careful."

"I am." He took a bite of sandwich with his free hand. "I'll walk you ladies upstairs when we're through eating."

Olivia released his hand. "All right."

Jonathan gathered the coffee cups from the table, wondering at Maggie's silence. The chatterbox had eaten her lunch without saying anything, but all the while looking from Belinda to Olivia, then back to Belinda again.

To his surprise, Belinda accompanied them to the surgical floor. And to his greater surprise, his and Olivia's hands met and grasped together until the two of them took their seats in the waiting room.

"Excuse me, I'm going to the ladies' room." Belinda went down the hall.

As soon as Belinda had left the area, Olivia turned to face them. "You two are the best friends I've got in the world, and I thank God you're here."

Jonathan slipped an arm around her, as did Maggie. Olivia leaned into him. "Hey, Sam's going to be all right. I'm praying for his healing, you know. And he even prayed with me last night."

She sat up straight, sniffled, then blew her nose on the tissues Maggie offered her. "I know. I'm doing better about Dad. It's just that Belinda's my mother."

Olivia's mind reeled from her admission. Saying the words out loud made the facts loud and clear. For the past hour, her thoughts had whirled, but the primary one was, *I'm sitting across the table from my mother.*

"Your mother?" Maggie blurted. "Belinda? Why? Why now?"

"She and Dad reconnected on Facebook and he told her about his surgery. I guess the guilt racked her so bad she had to come back to visit." The words flew from Olivia's mouth like knives aimed at a target. One of them jabbed her conscience. "I'm sorry."

"She abandoned you." Jonathan clenched his jaw.

"I know, but— Well, Belinda's a Christian now, has been for a while. She told me she's been trying to figure out how to make things right for a long time. She told me that when she first left it was because she didn't think she had it in her to be a mother. She wanted more." Her head ached. Her spirit craved the solace of the chapel. Jonathan's arm around her shoulders suffused warmth throughout her.

Oh, Dad, I wish you were able to help me with this. Your good sense would come in handy right now.

I am with you always.... Peace, be still. Olivia felt a peace, deep down under the layer of worry about her father, the numb shock of meeting Belinda and the emotions that wanted free rein. She held on to the knowledge as if it were an anchor.

Thank You, God, for the reminder. I am so hardheaded. She continued to wait in silence, grateful for her best friend and the man she loved on either side of her.

The man she loved. With a rush of longing, Olivia looked into Jonathan's dark eyes. She could lose herself in his gaze, which told her nothing in the world mattered to him except her.

A *pock-pock* of heels made Olivia watch Belinda approach them. She and Dad were complete opposites. Belinda carried herself like a former runway model, every detail of her wardrobe coordinated down to the leather pumps. How did this odd couple match up?

With lithe grace, Belinda settled into the vinyl seat across from Olivia. "Oh, I wish they'd tell us something soon."

"Yes, it's been a long morning," Olivia conceded. A nurse wearing scrubs covered with fluorescent cartoon cats entered the alcove.

"Is Samuel Shea's family here?"

"That's us, yes." Olivia stood, smoothing nonexistent wrinkles from her jeans. A warm hand grasped hers. Belinda. Olivia felt as if she were starring in a movie of the week; things like this didn't happen to regular people. But she didn't pull away from the elegant stranger.

"Your father's in recovery now, and he came through the surgery very well. We're moving him to his room soon, so I'll let you know when you can see him for a few minutes." The nurse smiled at them and left.

Olivia released the pent-up breath and looked at Belinda. "They'll let us see him. You were going to see him, right?"

Belinda let go of Olivia's hand. She fumbled with the simple gold chain on her neck. "I—I suppose so. I'm more nervous seeing him, I think, than seeing you. Not that I wasn't nervous seeing you." She sighed.

Maggie plucked at Olivia's elbow. "I'm—I'm going to leave now. I wanted to know for sure you were okay."

"We are. And we will be." They hugged. "I'll call you later?" No doubt Maggie would have more questions.

Jonathan moved to follow Maggie, but Olivia reached for his arm. "Jon, thanks for coming. Except you don't have to leave. I'm sure Dad will want to see you, too."

"All right."

Olivia realized she still clutched Jonathan's arm. A muscle tightened beneath his sleeve. "I'm glad you're here. I know it's been an—an awkward past few weeks."

"We're friends." His warm gaze studied her hand. "That will never change."

"I know." Her throat went dry.

He surprised her by pulling her close and kissing her on the forehead. "Good." She wanted to settle into the comfort of his arms, but stepped back slowly.

The nurse returned, and Olivia was glad to follow the woman. She breathed deeply before walking into the recovery room. Jonathan and Belinda followed so close that if Olivia stopped, they'd trample her heels.

Her father lay quietly, eyes closed. Machines monitored his pulse and breathing. Olivia reached for the bed rail and felt her fingers close around Jonathan's hand instead. Belinda moved to the other side of the bed.

Her mother said nothing, but the silent tears sliding down the woman's cheeks said much. Either that, or Belinda was a good actress. The spark of rage threatened to ignite once again, but Olivia fought it off. Not now, not here. She needed to focus on her father.

"Dad, hey." Olivia swallowed past the throb in her throat. "We're here. Me and Jonathan, and Belinda."

Her father's eyelids fluttered, then opened. Olivia caught the familiar twinkle he reserved for his girl. "I only had my lung operated on. I'm not blind, girl." Then he seemed to focus on the woman standing on his other side. "Lindy...you came... there's so much..." Her father's throat bobbed as he swallowed.

"I know."

"But stay...stay at the house, please." He swallowed again.

"Shh, don't talk." Olivia leaned over the bed and kissed her father on the cheek. "Rest. I'll make sure Belinda's settled in at the house. We'll have plenty of time to talk later."

He gave a slight nod. "I'll be back on the boat in a week or two. Isn't that right, Jon?"

"Yeah, I hope soon, Sam. But it'll likely be longer than that. Winter's coming, and you can't catch a cold."

Olivia's father's voice came out in a faint rasp. "That so? I'm not an infant you got to keep bundled up."

Belinda gave a soft chuckle. "You haven't changed, Sam."

Jonathan left after a few more minutes, too quickly for Olivia's liking. She felt tongue-tied now that just she and her mother remained at her father's bedside. The nurse assured them her father would be in ICU for a day or two, then moved to a regular floor before his release.

They stepped back into the hall.

"Well—" Olivia sighed "—I need to go by the office and let them know I'll be bringing some work home the next few weeks."

"I'll come by the house, too, if you don't mind, Liv."

"No, I don't."

"I just didn't want it to seem like I'm trying to barge in."

They ambled down the corridor to the elevators, the hub-bub of hospital traffic surrounding them.

"Do you have plans for this evening?" Belinda pulled a set of keys from her purse. "I was hoping we could have dinner somewhere."

"Well, I suppose so. I need to run by the lab and get some things from my office. I could meet you at the Sea Dawg."

Olivia bit her lip. She wasn't ready to let Belinda into the house.

"Oh, okay, then. I'll see you later, Liv."

Belinda walked to a sleek sedan, then Olivia heard the chirp of the alarm being disarmed. Olivia stalked to her car and let her tears flow before leaving the parking lot. Mom. Here again. So close and yet so far, all these years.

She realized one thing, though. Her first instinct hadn't been to call Frank; instead, she'd wanted Jonathan's comfort.

Chapter 14

"Your father told me about what happened to Robby O'Leary. I'm sorry." Belinda moved as though she wanted to reach across the table and touch Olivia's hand. The Saturday evening dinner crowd at the Sea Dawg bustled around them, yet Belinda seemed oblivious to the stares directed at them.

"Thank you." Olivia took a sip of her soda. "I suppose he told you I'd left Fairport for a while."

Her mother nodded. "Losing your father was always one of my worst fears. We were so young, younger than you and Robby even. To think you lost him a month before your wedding."

"Even if Robby had lived, there probably wouldn't have been a wedding after all." Olivia's cheeks flamed. "I'd already lost him without realizing it."

"Are you seeing someone now?"

"Yes…no…I'm not sure." Olivia didn't care to explain. "It's complicated."

Belinda smiled. "Ah, that nice guy I met at the hospital. Jonathan, was it?"

"Um…Jonathan's a great friend, but there's Frank." She shrugged.

Her mother's eyebrows creased. "Oh, my mistake. I hope you'll tell me about this other man."

"Frank teaches third grade at the elementary school. When Dad gets home from the hospital, Frank is taking me for a beach walk and then lunch at The Grog. Frank's hoping to remind me to still have fun, even though Dad's been sick." She avoided Belinda's puzzled gaze.

"Hmm…Frank doesn't mind Jonathan coming around? From what I can see, Jonathan's crazy about you."

"A relationship between Jonathan and me? Well, it wouldn't work. I can't be with someone who has such a risky profession. I don't want to lie awake nights, wondering if he's safe and warm, or if he's in trouble." The words poured out, surprising Olivia.

"So you don't think the Lord can take care of Jonathan better than you?"

"That's not what I meant."

"Liv, I said those same words. I worried about your father, pulling in those lobster pots, wondering if an arm or a leg would get caught in the lines and he'd get pulled over the side." Belinda leaned forward in her chair. "It took me many years to realize I was putting myself in a position above the Lord. I didn't think He could take care of Sam. Don't toss away a chance with a wonderful man who obviously loves you."

"I like Frank. No, I'm not in love with him. I'll admit that. But he's a good man." Olivia fumed at the patronizing expression on Belinda's face. The woman knew nothing about her. Nothing at all.

"Why do I hear hesitation in your voice? I really don't know you very well, Liv, but I've worked in real estate long enough to know that sound in a potential buyer's voice, the tone that tells me they're not sure about what they see." Belinda tapped

Olivia's hand with her manicured finger. "Take this one bit of free advice: don't sign the papers if you think you're settling for something other than what you really want in your deepest heart of hearts."

"Well, we're just friends. We've known each other a little more than a month."

"Fine, I'll back off." But Belinda said the words with a smile.

"Thank you." Olivia continued, "Tell me more about your life—after you left Fairport." Olivia would let her take a turn in the hot seat.

Belinda briefly hesitated. "I headed for California, and what I thought was adventure. I was *so* immature. I went through my savings quickly, then got a job answering the phone in a real estate office. Eventually I started selling real estate myself. My mother became ill, so I headed back east to be close to her about five years ago. I've been near Boston ever since."

"But you never contacted Dad."

"No, not until a few weeks ago. I know God was dealing with me to come home, but I put it off for so long. It was easier to think that…you were both better off without me. I was a lousy mom, selfish back then. I'd rather run with my friends than watch you. I was always leaving you with him, with my mother, whoever I could find. You were what they now call a 'spirited child,' and I didn't know how to handle you. No excuse, you were just a little one. And I was awful to your father before I left. We'd married so very young…." Belinda sighed.

"When did you become a Christian?"

"About three years ago."

Olivia nodded. They were in a public place. She didn't want to provide any more grist for the town's rumor mill than necessary. Olivia curbed back the words that wanted to come.

Since her dad's illness, she'd been going to the Bible more than ever for help concerning her reactions to others. Ephesians admonished her to be "tenderhearted, forgiving one another." Could she put herself in her mother's shoes and put her own feelings aside for a moment? What did it cost this woman to return to her husband and daughter without knowing the reception she'd receive?

"Has becoming a Christian made a difference in your life?" Olivia asked aloud.

"Yes, it has." Belinda's brown eyes moistened. "God's forgiven me. But I've realized I need to bridge this gap between us—me, you, your dad." Her gaze shifted to the checked tablecloth. "So what I'm asking is, will you forgive me? Please?"

"Do you know what it was like, watching my friends come home to moms who made cookies and read stories and went to school programs and taught them to put on makeup? That Dad didn't do those things and he was gone lots of the time? I had more babysitters that I could count when I was little until Mrs. Flaherty moved in next door." Olivia blinked back tears. She couldn't remember Belinda as her mother.

"My poor sweet girl." Belinda shook her head. "I was so wrong. So selfish. I can't go back, but will you at least consider being my friend?" She sniffed and dabbed her eyes with a tissue, gold bracelets catching the lights.

"For Dad, I'll try." Today they'd picked at old scabbed-over wounds that had never healed. From this point on, Olivia would focus on doing what she could to help her father get better. If it meant letting Belinda into her life, she'd do it.

Her mother changed the subject. "I'll be here when he's released from the hospital. If—if you don't mind, I'd like to come to the house and help."

"Of course. You and Dad are still married, right?"

Belinda nodded. "I grew up Catholic, and divorce was out of the question. So, your father and I are still married. On paper."

They finished their meals and passed on dessert. Belinda yawned into one hand, and Olivia understood. "I'm tired, too. I was up early to get to the hospital, and it's been a long day." Olivia picked up their check.

"I could have gotten that."

"No, this time is my treat. You've taken time out of what must be a busy schedule to be here."

Belinda removed a business card from a slim gold case and wrote on the back of it. "Here. I know your father opened the house to me, but I'm staying at the Seacliff Inn. Here's my number."

They went to their cars, and Belinda gave her a quick hug before they went their separate ways. Olivia left for home, anticipating the sanctuary and quiet. Dad had said to let Belinda stay with them, but truthfully, Olivia wasn't up to that. Too much too soon. Maybe later. Fortunately, Belinda had realized that.

She collected the mail from the mailbox, then checked the house phone voice mail. Maggie had called, assuring her she and Todd had been praying. Then Jonathan called, letting her know the same. Frank had called, reminding her of their plans for next weekend.

Her mother's words came back to her. Jonathan loved her, and she was trying to place herself above God. Absurd. Olivia's Bible lay on the kitchen table. She put the kettle on the stove to heat water for tea, then opened the Bible. She knew within seconds she could be reading verses that showed God's care and protection over His people. Then she could read verses about forgiveness.

There was the tricky part. Forgiving her mother. She heard Belinda's voice asking for forgiveness. Then Olivia's mind flashed back over the months, the memory of seeing Frances O'Leary at the supermarket resurfacing. Frances refused to forgive her. She could still see the fury and bitterness carved into the woman's face, eating her from the inside out.

Olivia could very well turn out the same way. Her heart thudded. "No, Lord, I don't want that to happen. I'm angry at my mother for leaving, angry that she's returned at such a difficult time. And maybe I am angry that You allowed her to come back now. Please, help me forgive her. I know You've forgiven her, just like You've forgiven me.

"I believe You're healing my father even now. And I would hate for any bitterness on my part toward my mother to grieve Dad. If I have to accept Your strength every day to help me, I will. Lord, I'm not strong enough to handle this on my own."

The shrieking teakettle punctuated the end of her prayer. Olivia kept a reverent silence as she brewed a cup of tea, feeling a stillness in the house. No matter what lay ahead concerning her parents, if the Lord was strengthening her, she could handle it.

After seeing Olivia at the hospital, Jonathan made some repairs on the boat and ordered his supplies for the next trip. Without much else to do, he ended up at Todd's charter office drinking coffee, then at Todd and Maggie's for supper.

"I wish Olivia wasn't being so pigheaded." Maggie waddled to a chair in the den and lowered herself onto the cushion.

"Hey, she's been through a lot lately." Jonathan sprang to her defense.

"I know that." Maggie glowered. "I meant about you two. Am I not right, honey?"

Todd looked up from the fireplace after he placed a piece of wood on the grate. He grinned. "I won't say you're wrong."

"Really, though," Maggie continued, "I believe the Lord has brought you two together."

"I think He needs to convince Olivia of that." Jonathan drew a deep breath. "I know she's been spending lots of time with Frank, but I'm not staying out of the picture."

Todd stood and stretched, a look of contemplation on his face. "What if I hired you to pilot one-day fishing tours? You know I'm swamped in the high season. Maybe that's a way to compromise."

"Thanks, but I won't sacrifice my dream because of her fears. Maybe I sound cold, but I can't do it. And—" he gave

Todd a punch on the arm "—you aren't busy enough right now to afford another captain."

Todd nodded. "I figured you'd see it that way. So, there's only one solution I can see right now."

"Yes." Jonathan's gut clenched at the thought of Olivia and what might be. "We can pray."

They prayed for Olivia and her parents, plus Jonathan.

After the amen, Jonathan cleared his throat. "Thanks."

"No problem," Todd said. "We're supposed to encourage each other."

Jonathan smiled. "Well, I appreciate it." He reached for his jacket.

He headed home, feeling a peace about his relationship with Olivia, a peace he hadn't possessed in a long time. "Thank You, Lord. I'm going to keep trusting You about Liv. I love her. I'll wait for her. Somehow, in the meantime, I'll convince her she belongs with me."

Chapter 15

"Just let me sleep in the recliner. I'll be fine until I can go up and down stairs." Olivia's father had his jaw set, brows furrowed. Yet his features remained pale.

"Have it your way, Sam." Belinda walked briskly to the kitchen, leaving Olivia and her father in the entryway.

Olivia tried to support her dad as he walked to the recliner, but he shrugged off her assistance. "I'll make it. I need to do this myself."

The doorbell rang. "I'll be right back, Dad."

Frances O'Leary stood outside, a foil-covered pan in her hands. "I brought you some meat loaf. My own recipe."

"Thanks." Olivia felt a surge of compassion. "Dad came home today. And my...my mom's here. Would you like to come in?"

The older woman smiled, her face losing some of its hardness. "I can't today. I'm on the way to the shop. But I will sometime."

"Good. And I'll drop your pan off when we're through. Thank you."

Frances nodded, stepping off the porch. "That'll be fine." She turned and strode briskly to her idling car at the curb.

Olivia closed the door, balancing the pan of meat loaf on her arm. "That was Frances O'Leary. She brought her special meat loaf."

Her father groaned.

Belinda emerged from the kitchen. She'd put on an apron, and Olivia wondered where her mother had found the relic. "Oh, meat loaf sounds perfect. We can save that for supper tonight if you two would like."

Olivia laughed. "You'd better have a backup plan, like take-out."

"I don't remember her meat loaf being that bad." Belinda accepted the pan from Olivia. She went back to the kitchen. Olivia heard the refrigerator door open and close. "And anyway—" Belinda called out "—we can smother it with ketchup."

Dad's laugh rang out. Then he began to cough.

"Don't overdo it, Dad."

"I'll be fine. Don't look so worried."

Olivia picked up his overnight bag. "I'll try not to. But if you have a hard time breathing, speak up." First thing, before Frank picked her up, she'd do some laundry.

The mountain of clothes had grown in front of the washing machine in the cellar. Olivia allowed the ordinary mundane chore to relax her. Socks and whites into one pile, darks and colors into another pile, towels into a third. She tossed the whites into the washer and watched the steam rise from the hot water.

Why wasn't life so easily sorted out? Olivia settled onto the bottom step of the cellar stairs and listened to Belinda's feet puttering back and forth from the kitchen above.

A sense of not-quite-right niggled in her head, the uncomfortable knowledge that her mother was assimilating herself into their home routine. Ever since the surgery, she hadn't had a chance to speak with her father about Belinda.

Adding to the pile of trouble was the matter of her father's lobster pots. Every day Isadore Pappalardo either called or stopped by the house with an update or a check for the catch. They couldn't count on his kindness indefinitely, and she didn't know when her father could go back to work. She needed to speak with her father about a lot of things.

A man's dreams could die in an instant. Jonathan glared at the uncooperative engine, while his crew stared at him. *Isabella* was stocked and ready to go, except the engine was dead in the water.

He tossed the wrench into the toolbox, stood and faced the men. "I'm sorry. Looks like we're stuck here for now."

"Barrotta, I can't afford this. I got kids to feed," one of the younger men said.

"Don't worry," offered Stumpy. "I got word that Skip Callahan's got a place or two on his boat. Leaves tomorrow." The older man tossed his rucksack over one shoulder. "Sorry, Jon. Give me a holler when you're back in action." The two men clomped off the boat and strode from the dock.

His last remaining crew member, Jeff, a young man barely out of high school, remained. "Man, what a bad break. But if I can give you a hand, let me know." Jonathan nodded, and watched Jeff leave, as well.

Alone, he stared at the engine. Pete had advised him he might be able to coax the engine through the winter, but to plan for a replacement come spring. Trouble was, he didn't think the bank would lend him more funds for another engine.

He sank to his knees before the engine hold. "God, I'm in trouble now. If I can't get this engine going again or get another one, I might as well sell this rig now. You've brought me this far. Keep me going."

Liv's sweet face came to mind. What would she think of him, landlocked until he figured out a way to ship out again? Maybe she would hound him to go full-time with woodworking.

But he was kidding himself. She wouldn't worry about him. What woman would want a man who was a failure? All he knew how to do was fish and build things. Liv was better off with someone like Frank, stable with a steady job and income. She didn't need the uncertainty of a fisherman's life. The knowledge had a bitter taste. Jonathan expelled a sigh.

He had promised the Lord he would wait for Olivia. Maybe he'd been wrong about that, too. Yet he hadn't mistaken the peace he'd received in prayer.

His head ached. "Lord, it's me again." He sighed and rubbed his forehead. "I don't see how You can work out this mess. But I'd appreciate Your showing me."

Jonathan stood. He needed an engine expert. Sam Shea came to mind first. Except today Sam was coming home from the hospital. Either he'd be tired or glad for the company. Jonathan would call later to see if he could talk to Sam.

He closed the engine hold and eyed the items in the galley. Maybe someone else would buy his perishable supplies.

Shouts outside brought Jonathan to the deck. A lobster boat was heading straight for the *Isabella*. The slumped figure at the helm leaned to one side, and the boat's course diverted, but not enough.

The impact sent Jonathan sprawling. The *Isabella* tugged on her moorings but held fast. Jonathan leaped to his feet and jumped to the dock.

Other fishermen had beat him to the lobster boat, where a grizzled older man lay bewildered on its deck. Helping hands lifted him to his feet. Another man had shut down the engine before the boat careened around the harbor anymore.

"Isadore Pappalardo!" a man shouted. "Stubborn old fool. You should know better than to pull your pots in when you have the flu."

Jonathan inspected the *Isabella* for any visible damage, but thankfully Isadore's boat had slammed into her sideways instead of head-on. The wayward lobster boat was moved to another place on the dock.

Of course Isadore had continued hauling pots in despite having the flu. Fishermen didn't get sick days. And besides, Isadore was helping Sam. Jonathan needed to call Sam more than ever. His current troubles put aside for the moment, Jonathan rushed from the docks.

The surf roared in their ears as Olivia and Frank walked the wintry beach, vacant that late afternoon except for the two of them. No matter the season, Olivia felt drawn to the shore, the rhythmic waves soothing her soul. She found a few shells, and allowed them to be swept back into the waves.

Today was Frank's promised beach walk, then a drive to a country inn for lunch. Olivia was glad for the excuse to give her parents some time to themselves, even though it was her father's first day home. She kept her cell phone handy in her purse, ready to accept voice mail messages in case of an emergency. But she had left, with Belinda encouraging her to go and have a good time with Frank.

"What are you thinking so deeply about?" Frank snapped her attention back to him.

"Today, being here, my parents..." She shivered as a gust bit through her wool coat. He reached for her hand. She moved away from him and reached for a shell on the sand. Olivia scolded herself. What did she think he'd meant by a beach walk? Why had she agreed?

"You've been going through a lot lately."

"It's been interesting, to say the least."

"I couldn't imagine. Liv, I've been praying for you, and about you...about us..." Frank captured her hand, stopped walking and turned her to face him.

Her pounding pulse dulled the surf's roar. She couldn't think of what to say. They were just friends, at least to her. Of course she'd contemplated more. And more, with his intense brown eyes, was staring her in the face.

"I appreciate your prayers. Dad's doing so much better and I'm learning to get used to Belinda being around. Most of the time." Now she was babbling. "I've been learning about forgiveness, especially seeing things from Frances's point of view. To see someone who you believe has caused so much pain—"

He silenced her with a gloved finger on her lips. "I did pray for your dad's health, and for your family, but what I wanted to talk to you about was our relationship. Olivia, you're beautiful, intelligent, strong—"

He leaned closer, his mouth moving closer toward hers. She pulled away. "No, please don't."

Frank stepped back. "What is it? Did I move too quickly? I know, I probably shouldn't have tried to kiss you."

"I—" Olivia sighed.

"It's all right. I apologize." A frown clouded his features to match the day. "We should be heading to the restaurant anyway." Frank turned back for the car.

They lunched at an elegant inn farther inland, leaving the smell of the sea behind them. The potatoes and clams in Olivia's chowder looked delicious but seemed tasteless. Then her stomach ached while she and Frank poked through an antique store on the way home.

"Are you feeling okay?" Although his mood remained somber, he touched her elbow in concern.

"My stomach is acting up." Olivia felt queasy.

"We can go now if you'd like." Frank held up an old picture of a mother and child. "Isn't this a great picture?"

Olivia's jumbly stomach stilled itself for a moment. "It's beautiful." The gilded frame held a reproduction of a Mary Cassatt painting of a young mother, who looked very much like Maggie, holding a small child and bathing her little feet.

Olivia looked at the price. "This is impractical, but Maggie would love it." She bought the picture before she changed her mind. "Now I'm ready to go if you are."

They headed along the shoreline road, Olivia keeping silent for most of the trip. No matter how much she tried to convince herself otherwise, she couldn't replace her affection for Jonathan. It wasn't fair to Frank either.

"Frank…" She wanted to find the right words. "I don't know how to say this."

He didn't take his focus from the road. "Take your time."

"I'm sorry, but…" She inhaled sharply. "I can't see you anymore. I mean, we shouldn't go out. I wasn't trying to lead you on."

Frank nodded slowly. "I was wondering if this might happen."

"There's someone else—"

"Jonathan Barrotta."

"I was trying hard to forget him. And you're a wonderful, kindhearted man." She felt as if she were rubbing salt in Frank's wound.

A muscle worked in Frank's jaw.

"I know there's a special someone for you, Frank. I don't know what the Lord has in store for me, but I can't…I can't forget about Jonathan. I'm sorry." Olivia sighed.

"We're still friends, though, right?" His warm gaze met hers.

"Yes, we are."

"I'll be all right. This is my fault, trying to make more of what should only be a friendship." Frank downshifted as they headed into downtown Fairport. The dwindling sunlight broke through a few clouds.

Please, Lord, show me the light in this bleak situation. I feel terrible about hurting Frank. Forgive me. And I can't just run back to Jonathan. Not if I can't get over this fear.

Jonathan knocked on the Sheas' front door. When Jonathan had explained about Isadore over the phone, Sam asked him to come right away.

Belinda Shea opened the door. "Hello, again, Jonathan." Her designer pantsuit looked out of place covered with an apron. Jonathan followed her to the living room, where Sam sat in his recliner, breathing into a little plastic piece that attached to a box by some plastic tubing.

Sam lifted the mouthpiece from his lips. "Jon, sit down and we'll talk in a few." He replaced the mouthpiece and slowly inhaled.

"Coffee, Jonathan?" Belinda called from the kitchen.

"Sure."

Sam shifted to a more upright position in his chair. "Now, you say Isadore's come down with the flu and he's not pulling his pots in?"

"Yeah. And plus, his boat's out of commission for a while. He rammed the *Isabella*. She's okay, except for her engine."

"Okay. Yeah." Sam nodded. "Sounds like you're in a bit of a pickle yourself. Do you still have a crew?"

Jonathan sighed. "I will, once I get the engine either repaired or replaced."

Sam nodded and appeared to think for a moment. "And here I am, housebound."

"I hope you'll soon be feeling better." Jonathan accepted the cup of coffee from Belinda. "Thanks, um, Mrs. Shea."

"Call me Belinda. And you're welcome." She smiled and sat on the sofa.

Sam turned off the breathing machine. "Okay. I tell you what, Jon. We can help each other out."

"Okay…"

"I've got some rainy day money put away. And I've got lobster pots that need hauling in. You see to my lobsters until I can get back to work, or Isadore can work for me, and I'll make sure you get that engine, son."

Jonathan blinked. "Sam, I don't know what to say." He hadn't planned on asking for help, or finding himself responsible for Sam's lobster pots. And who knew how long he'd have to work for Sam before the man could take his own boat out again? Or if Isadore would agree to help Sam again?

To his logical mind, it seemed like he'd be wasting his time. Yet Sam needed him, and Jonathan couldn't refuse the man in his need.

Chapter 16

For the past two weeks, Olivia had welcomed the work to keep herself busy, the last rush for data before the whales headed south for the winter.

Dad regained his strength every day. Belinda had set up a small office in the entryway to conduct her business. Jonathan came around after checking her dad's lobster pots. Olivia usually managed to find a reason to stay in her room when Jonathan stopped by the house. She would steel her heart from him. Ironic, she realized, as they puttered along in the boat, her avoidance did little to quell her fears for Jonathan.

"Liv, hold the tiller steady!" Rusty, Olivia's colleague, bobbed up and down as he aimed the crossbow at the humpback whale floating yards from their steel-bottomed inflatable raft.

"I'm trying to!" Her throbbing wrists and white-knuckled fingers held the tiller on the outboard motor.

Rusty gritted his teeth. "If I don't get these tags implanted today, I won't have a chance until spring. This is the last pod of whales in the area." The tiny harpoon tipped with a small electronic tag zipped from the bow and landed firmly in the outer part of the whale's thick skin.

Olivia bit her lip. "You're sure that doesn't hurt her?"

"She's fine. Not much more than a pinch." Rusty fitted another dart with a device intended to snatch a sample of the whale's tissue.

"Ooh. Spotter, I'm sorry." Olivia held her breath as Rusty used the harpoon to grab a sample from the whale's skin. The transmitter linked to a satellite would tell them where the whales went; hopefully the specimens Olivia gathered would tell them more about the mysterious life of the whales, too.

She let Rusty take the tiller and moved to put the scrapings into glass vials. "You're sure this is no worse than sloughing off skin cells?"

"Don't worry, Spotter will forgive you."

They puttered back to the main boat, anchored in the waters of Stellwagen Bank.

After they docked at the institute, Olivia gathered some data files and printouts, left the plankton with a lab tech and headed home.

Frances O'Leary's meat loaf pan clanked against a coffee mug on the floor of the car. Olivia had meant to return the pan to Frances over a week ago, but instead it ended up traveling around town with her. She should stop at Frances's gift shop on the way home.

She pulled up behind Frances's Buick, which was parked in front of the downtown store. "Here we go." The sign on the front of the store had been turned to closed, but Olivia saw Frances cross the showroom floor to unlock the glass door.

"Olivia, how are you?" Frances wore a guarded expression as she let Olivia inside the store. Her gaze darted from Olivia's face to the metal loaf pan, then to the floor.

"Busy, but fine otherwise. Here's your pan. I've been meaning to return it." Olivia regarded the older woman for a moment. "Frances, would you like to grab a cup of coffee with me?"

"No." The word shot from Frances's mouth like a dart. "I mean, not tonight." She sighed deeply, as if expelling a life's worth of heaviness.

"Are you all right? How can I help?" Olivia asked. Part of her wanted to flee the tirade to come. Another part glimpsed loneliness in the woman's eyes. And tears.

"I owe you an apology." Frances inhaled. Tears streamed from her carefully made-up eyes. "There's so much I could say, but I've said so much in the past I don't think I could make up for the pain I caused you."

"You don't have to say anything," Olivia began.

"Yes, I do. For years and years, I've prided myself on being a Christian woman. A pillar of the church. No matter what came my way, I'd emerge with my head held high. And then I lost Robby and blamed you. I talked about you almost every chance I had. When you left, I was glad. I hoped you'd never come back. That way you couldn't remind me of my pain.

"Then you came home this past summer, and I felt like I'd lost my son all over again. But—" Frances drew yet another ragged breath "—it's not your fault, Liv. I tried so hard to hold Robby tight and make sure he was okay that he slipped through my fingers anyway. The Bible study I attend has been learning what real trust in God means. And I see I haven't. Not really ever."

Olivia laid a hand on Frances's arm. "I forgive you. I won't hold the past against you." Now she was crying, too. "I know you're lonely, and I'm sorry, too. I should have tried to love you after we lost Robby, and I pulled away."

"We both did."

"Please, we should get together for coffee one night. Life has been rather interesting lately."

Frances smiled, and Olivia noticed its loveliness. "I think I'd like that. Oh, one more thing."

"Yes?"

"Don't let your fear keep you from missing out on a blessing." Frances gave Olivia a quick hug. "We can't control many things in our lives, but we know someone who does."

Olivia nodded. "Thanks."

"I mean it. Think about it."

"Stay for supper, Jon." Belinda placed another plate on the table without waiting for Jonathan's answer.

"Well, since you're twisting my arm, sure." His stomach rumbled at the smell of stew. And Olivia's mother had made enough for a small army, judging by the size of the stockpot on the stove.

Sounds from the front of the house told Jonathan that Olivia had arrived home from the lab. He braced himself for her reaction to his presence. For two weeks he'd been hauling in Sam's lobsters, with an occasional hand from a fellow lobsterman. Either Olivia made herself scarce when he visited Sam, or she would be gone. Jonathan reminded himself to be patient.

Frank Pappalardo didn't sit with Olivia in church anymore, a fact that hadn't escaped Jonathan. Yet she still showed no inclination to be anything more than friends with Jonathan.

"Hi, I'm home." Olivia stopped short of the dining room. "Jonathan, hi." He saw her note the number of plates on the table.

"Supper's ready. You two dish up your stew, and I'll get your dad's bowl." Belinda moved through the tiny kitchen with familiarity. Jonathan saw Olivia's expression turn into a thundercloud. Her mother took a tray to the living room.

"How are things?" Jonathan gestured toward the living room with his head.

"Oh, I don't know." Olivia spooned some stew into a bowl. She lowered her voice and continued. "I go back and forth between wanting to rage at her, and other times I want to know what it's like to have a mom. The coward's come home. But then, that's just what I did." She gave him a lopsided smile. "For Dad's sake, I go with the flow."

He rested a hand on her shoulder. "You look tired."

"I am." A line formed between her brows. "Rusty told me to take some time off, to work on my thesis. The pods are leaving for the winter, so all I have to do is study data and write until spring. Plus, be available if a school wants to schedule a presentation."

"So, you'll be home, then?"

"That's the idea. I can be near Dad. He still thinks he's Superman." They moved to the table; Belinda, Jonathan supposed, had decided to remain in the living room with her husband.

"Yeah, he's pretty super to lug those pots in by himself. One false move, and he could be over the side with one of those heavy wire pots taking him to the bottom. And I thought I had a hard job!" Jonathan's arms throbbed from pulling in the lobster pots. He needed to pick up some liniment on the way home.

Olivia frowned. "Yes, it's dangerous to work a lobster boat alone." She nibbled some of her stew, then played with the spoon. "That's why I want to help you."

"Help me?" Jonathan crossed his arms in front of his chest.

"I want to pilot Dad's boat while you pull in the pots. We can get the job done more quickly and safely than someone going it alone."

"Liv, I don't need your help."

"I can't study all the time, and I can't rattle around the house all day." She hissed the words across the table at him. "Besides, I've…" She stopped and slumped back in her chair.

"You've what?" Jonathan leaned forward in his chair.

She swallowed hard. "I've missed you. And I've been wrong to avoid you."

He allowed a smile to spread across his face. "So you *have* missed me. I was beginning to think I'd come down with a contagious disease."

"No." She shook her head. Olivia met his eyes, a determined expression on her face. "Frances O'Leary taught me not to let unforgiveness eat me away inside."

"Yet you want to pilot the boat to get away from your mother."

"Yeah, I'm contradicting myself, I know. I'm taking this one step at a time." Olivia's eyes were full of hope. Something passed between them, and Jonathan wanted to at least take her hand. She still loved him; that much he knew. If she needed to get out of the house, he couldn't deny her the chance to be with him.

"All right. If your dad doesn't mind, then I'll come by for you in the morning." When she looked at him like that, how could he tell her no?

Chapter 17

"I've got to go to Boston for a few days on business," Belinda announced on a Friday morning in mid-November. She wore one of her tailored suits, her hair swept back into a sleek knot at the back of her head.

Good. Olivia gulped down some coffee and prepared some extra for the big thermos. *I could use a break from the mothering. I feel like I'm suffocating.*

"Okay." Olivia nonchalantly clomped along in an old pair of boots to the mudroom closet. Dad probably had some extra work gloves stashed somewhere. She needed to find them soon; Jonathan would arrive at any moment. Her heart sang and she reminded herself she had nothing to be nervous about.

"I was making sure you'd be around for your father this weekend. I don't think I'll be back until Monday night or lunchtime Tuesday." She shuffled through some papers in her leather case.

"Don't worry about us. We'll be fine." She waved Belinda

away with assurances, and tried not to sigh with relief when her mother's sedan disappeared down the street.

Her father was reading the paper when she came into the living room. "Hey, Dad. How's it going this morning?"

His gray hair hung limp from a recent shower, but he had a sparkle in his eye she hadn't seen in months. "I'm doing okay. I'm worn out from the trip up and down stairs, but I'll get there. Jonathan's coming by for you?"

"Yes." Olivia went for her coffee cup on the kitchen table. "Hopefully we'll get a good price at the market."

"Hope so. The season's over at the end of December. Six more weeks before we shut down 'til April." Sam laid the paper on his lap.

Olivia nodded. "I think it's wonderful what you're doing for Jon. Helping him get that engine he needs."

"He's a good man, Liv. He's smart, a fast learner. Wish I could talk 'im into going into business with me." She felt her father's probing gaze follow her from the living room.

"He's got his own boat, Dad." She had resigned herself to that fact. Worry had caused her to volunteer to help him. Was she making a mistake?

A firm knock sounded on the door before it opened. Jonathan entered the living room. "Hey, Liv, you ready? G'morning, Sam." He wore several layers of clothing topped by a wool plaid jacket.

"Morning, son. Take care of my girl and my boat."

Olivia grabbed the thermos, then passed through the living room. "Dad!" Her face had probably bloomed red.

"Gladly, Sam." Then Jonathan winked at her.

Jonathan kept quiet as he steadied himself against the boat's movement. The *Lindy* moved parallel to the shoreline, headed toward the buoys marking Sam's lobster pots. Olivia's gaze was fixed on the dark gray water, her cheeks spotted red from the cold.

"I forgot how freezing it is out here." Her puffs of breath were snatched by the wind.

"Yeah, we'll be soaked through by the time we get home, even with these rubber waders." Jonathan eyed the bulky sweater Olivia wore. The waders bloomed out around her hips. It was all he could do not to take her in his arms and warm her up with a long-ago promised kiss. Yet their summer closeness seemed a distant memory. At least now she wasn't avoiding him.

"Here's one, right?" Olivia downshifted the boat into an idle.

"That's it." He studied the numbers on the marker. "You remember well."

She grinned for the first time that morning. "Dad would bring me out sometimes when I begged him. He taught me to drive the boat."

"I've missed you." The words came out before Jonathan could stop them. He glanced sideways at her capable figure clenching the helm with gloved hands. Somehow he and Olivia had landed side-by-side piloting a boat. "My feelings haven't changed all this time." He wanted to snatch the glove off his hand and caress Olivia's face and lose his fingers in her hair.

"I know."

Her look made Jonathan want to forget all about lobsters in traps beneath the frigid waters. He groaned as he headed toward the back of the boat. Today would be torturous, but he would survive.

Two more pots, and they'd be done for the day. Olivia shivered, hoping Jonathan hadn't noticed. When she got home, she'd reheat some lasagna and make them both some hot chocolate. He still cared. She knew that much, although being close to him every day for an entire week drove her crazy.

She'd been enjoying her trips out on her dad's boat, though it bore the nickname her father had given to Belinda. Since Belinda's return from Boston on Tuesday, they hadn't really conversed with each other. One week until Thanksgiving, when they were expected to portray a happy family.

Her cheeks burned from the cold, and from the recollection of her struggle to deal with Belinda, coupled with the memory of Jeremy's Sunday school lesson. They'd moved on to Ephesians 4, discussing relationships with family and friends. So far Olivia knew she'd struck out on many counts.

Get rid of all bitterness, rage, and anger...be kind and compassionate to one another, forgiving each other, just as in Christ God forgave you, repeated the verses in her mind. *I've been so wrong, Lord. Please forgive me. I'll do better from now on.* She needed to ask Belinda's forgiveness, as well. Her mother was trying. Humility was a tough road to walk.

Olivia held the boat steady and looked over her shoulder. Jonathan's massive arms hauled the rope onto the deck until up came the steel pot full of lobsters. It crashed onto the deck, and Jonathan skillfully measured each lobster before tossing it into the hold or over the side. He looked up at her. She'd been staring, and her stomach turned over on itself with the knowledge that he'd caught her.

"Give me a hand here." One corner of his mouth quirked up in a half grin.

She heard and obeyed, not caring that he'd called her to help him with a pot he could handle himself.

Olivia's boots slipped on the wet deck, and she skidded into the circle of Jonathan's arms. Heat radiated from his body, the warmth spreading to her despite the bright orange waders she wore.

"I need to grab the helm," she sputtered. "The boat's drifting."

"That doesn't matter right now." At his husky tones, Olivia's knees threatened to give way. Robby had never caused such a stirring inside her.

Olivia wanted to wriggle out of his embrace; Jonathan's eyes, brown and fathomless, held her still. Her fear had kept them apart. And she wouldn't open the door to love him without fear. Nor would she tempt herself with the promise of a future with Jonathan. Her fear would hold him captive, and she couldn't ask him to leave the life he loved. Jonathan deserved a better woman.

Too late. She tumbled into the fire that crackled from his expression. His lips lowered to hers and everything, the rocking boat, the lobsters in the hold, the lobster pot and its marker waiting to be tossed into the sea, lost its importance. The firmness and controlled passion of his kiss ignited her response. It didn't matter that his face had a day's worth of stubble, or that their waders squeaked in protest at the friction between them.

Jonathan was letting her return his kiss, and Olivia knew it. She pulled back enough to touch his jaw with a trembling hand. "You—you said you'd shave before you kissed me."

"It's a long time since summer. Guess I forgot." Then he kissed her again, as though reluctant to scratch her tingling cheeks.

Jonathan left her breathless. The cold air hit her face and lips. She shivered, and his embrace tightened.

"I love you," he whispered.

"And I love you." Pent-up tears released, blazing a hot trail on her cheeks. Olivia put her face on his chest; his gloved hand rubbed her head.

He forced her back to look at him. "Baby, you're all the woman I'll ever need. I've wanted to tell you that for years, since the Three Musketeers ran around together; there's never been anyone else."

Olivia studied his expression. How long had he loved her? Even when she had fallen in love with Robby? "That long? Why did you wait for me?"

"There was a time I'd resigned myself to the fact I'd lost you forever, when I saw you and Robby together." His grip loosened around her. "And then after we lost him, I'd hoped that one day…" He looked over her shoulder as if studying the steel lobster pot behind her.

"You need someone who's not afraid of your job, someone

who won't hinder you." She set her jaw. "I can't promise you I can learn to conquer this fear. I've tried."

Another spark ignited in his eyes. "That doesn't matter to me. I love you, just the way you are now. We can take it one step at a time." He peeled off a glove and ran a warm hand down her wet cheek. "If we love each other and trust the Lord, nothing's impossible."

Olivia stepped around him and headed for the helm. She wouldn't look at him. She'd been foolish to think she could work this closely with Jonathan and not be affected by him. If she said anything more, she could make things worse. No need to open her mouth. Olivia swallowed hard and let the wind dry her cheeks.

Jonathan's steps clomped back to the wire pot. Then came a splash. They'd be done soon but not quickly enough for her liking. His steps approached her again.

"You know what, Liv? I can get one of the guys from the crew to help me. Jeff could use the money. You and I won't have to see each other like this every day."

Olivia nodded. It would be better that way. Her aching heart told her she'd just lost another man to the sea.

Chapter 18

Jonathan placed the maple wood baby cradle in front of Todd and Maggie's fireplace, then topped it with a gigantic pink satin bow. He had stayed up late, sanding and finishing his masterpiece, rather than lying awake thinking of Olivia. "You think Maggie will like it?"

"Definitely." Todd nodded. "Hey, do you want to stick around? We've got tons of food, and there are leftovers from Thanksgiving. Besides, with all these women coming for the baby shower, I'm sorely outnumbered."

"You got a deal, man. I can handle it." Jonathan belied the apprehension in his gut by giving Todd a grin.

Olivia would be coming to the baby shower. He hadn't seen her since the day he'd kissed her on her father's boat. How many times had he woken up in the night wishing for a repeat kiss?

The hardheaded woman had to be fooling herself. He'd felt the response to his kiss and knew she held as deep a passion as he did. Yet passion and companionship weren't enough to cement a relationship together. Jonathan wanted mutual faith and trust, in each other and God.

Jonathan followed Todd to the kitchen, where Maggie was on her hands and knees, reaching into the back of a cabinet for something.

"Maggie! What do you think you're doing?" Todd bellowed and ran for the cabinet.

"I'm getting a tray for the crackers," came her muffled reply. "And don't scare me like that. I nearly bashed my head on the cabinet."

"Honey—" he reached for her waist "—you should have asked me for help. Or your mother. Where is she, by the way?"

"Upstairs, wrapping my gifts, she said." Maggie emerged, red-faced and blowing dust from a metal tray. "You know, nothing like the last minute and all. Hey, Jon! You here for the food? My mother has been cooking and preparing in overdrive for this spread she's laid out here."

"You bet." He poured a cup of coffee into a pink paper cup. "If you think you'll need help eating it, I'm your man." His stomach growled as he surveyed the trays of cold cuts, cheeses, potato chips and cut vegetables, and thought of his nearly empty refrigerator. "So how are you doing?"

"Other than feeling as big and round as that Santa at the mall, extremely fidgety because nobody will let me do anything, I'm fine." Maggie practically glowed.

Jonathan imagined Olivia would look even more beautiful if she were pregnant someday. Deep down, he still harbored a hope that she might return his love and not let fear give her such torment.

He and Todd made sandwiches and retreated to Todd and Maggie's combination exercise room and office. Why was he torturing himself for a chance to see Olivia?

They settled onto a pair of office chairs in front of Todd's computer screen.

"See?" Todd brought up a program. "I have all the charter

accounts on file. Come tax season, all I have to do is give a printout to my accountant and let her do the rest."

"Of course, you don't have much business this time of year."

Todd shook his head. "No, not really. I'm thinking of opening a machine shop, to fix boat engines for small craft. Speaking of engines, what's up with your boat?"

Jonathan didn't want to think about it. "Working for Sam, I've gotten an advance to help me with the engine. It should arrive any day now. The guys and I are going to make one more trip out." He dreaded the words to come. "My note is late at the bank."

"Jon, why didn't you say something, man? I could've chipped in to help."

"You've got a baby on the way, it's slow work for everybody this time of year. Nobody can spare the extra money." If Todd wasn't such a good friend, Jonathan couldn't bear the humiliation of being in dire financial straits.

"That's what we're here for." Todd punched his arm. "If you have a need, if I have a need, we should help each other. But I don't know if you don't tell me."

"I appreciate it. But we're leaving Monday. The men need the money, I've got bills to pay and the forecast looks good right now." Jonathan tried to appear confident. "Just pray we have a good trip, is all I ask."

The office door flew open. A woman from church poked her head in. "Hey, the ladies want to meet the carpenter."

"No, that's okay…" Jonathan began.

Todd gave him a shove. "Your public awaits."

Jonathan glared at his friend. "Oh, thanks. Just what I need." At least if he saw Olivia in the group, they wouldn't have any confrontations or words. He wanted to see her, and hoped she'd see the love in his eyes.

Olivia's heart thudded like a jackhammer when Jonathan entered the room. The women's applause drowned out the pounding in her ears. She felt Belinda squeeze one of her hands that rested on her lap.

"Are you all right?" Belinda whispered.

"Yes…" She watched as Jonathan answered questions and received some good-natured ribbing from Maggie.

"That man loves you. It's radiating all the way across the room."

"I know he does, but it's not enough." Olivia bit into a carrot stick, hating the sound of her own words.

"We'll talk about this on the way home, okay?"

Olivia nodded. Somehow, she'd get through the rest of the baby shower. Then her eyes locked with Jonathan's, and a wave of love washed over her.

Lord, I don't deserve him. I am cowardly and weak.

The remainder of the night was a blur. The painting reproduction she'd bought for the nursery made almost as big a hit as Jonathan's cradle did. One thing was for sure, Jonathan showed his love for his friends, another quality that made him hard to forget.

"We'll hang the picture right over the crib in the nursery." Maggie gave Olivia a hug with tears in her eyes, then whispered in her ear, "Two beautiful gifts from our two best friends."

Olivia and Belinda left after making sure Maggie didn't try to do the dishes herself. Once inside Belinda's sleek sedan, Olivia closed her eyes and leaned back on the leather seat.

"Maggie looked radiant tonight," Belinda observed. "I'm glad the last part of her pregnancy has gone so well. Just over two weeks now, is it, until her due date?"

"That's right." Olivia faced the window.

"I was glad to see Jonathan, too. Because Isadore is over the flu, your father has more help than he can handle with the lobsters. I'm forbidding him to go out until spring, though." Belinda gave a tiny laugh.

"Are you afraid?" She glanced at her mother.

"Mmm…sometimes, but not about your dad. I've had to

realize that Sam's Heavenly Father loves him so much more than I ever could. And I lo…" Her mother fell silent.

"You love him?"

Belinda nodded, the lights from an oncoming car revealing unshed tears. "Yes, I do. Very much. I wasted so many years running, so much time I could have had with both of you." She fell silent, and Olivia let the silence hang between them for a few minutes. Her own throat caught. But they couldn't rewind time. There were no do-overs.

Belinda sucked in a deep breath before continuing. "But I know that God is in control of what happens to Sam. No matter what I do. If He loves Sam, He'll do what's best for him. So I keep reminding myself of that fact. I kind of tend to take over and try to run things when it's not my responsibility."

Olivia grinned in the dark. How many times had she barged in and called the shots? Maybe she was more like her mother than she'd realized.

"So you're not trying to keep Dad off his boat because you're afraid, then?"

"No, it's for his health. He tends to be rather hardheaded."

"I've noticed that." Olivia found a laugh coming out, which turned into a groan. "Between your take-charge attitude and Dad's hardheadedness, I'm all set."

"Aw, c'mon. It's not that bad. I'm one of the top commercial real estate agents in the Boston area, thanks to the gift God's given me. The negative aspects of our personalities can be used for good things, you know, once we let God have control of our lives." Belinda turned the car into the driveway. "Listen to me, I'm getting preachy. Sorry. It's not my place."

"That's all right. I'm glad you came tonight. The other ladies seemed happy to see you." Olivia remembered what it had felt like that summer, trying to reenter a life she'd left behind. Only she hadn't been gone for decades. Compassion for Belinda surged through her. A mere flicker of anger at her mother's abandonment sputtered, then died.

Was it progress? Was she learning to love her mother and forgive her? Olivia hoped so.

Sleep refused to come that night. Jonathan lay awake instead, watching the lights of the harbor outside his apartment window.

What if by some chance, Olivia changed her mind and allowed herself to love him? What could he give her? He tossed the covers off and padded on the chilly hardwood floor to get a cup of instant coffee.

If things didn't improve, he'd end up losing both the apartment and the boat. At least the Jeep was paid for. Jonathan smirked as he put a cup of water in the microwave. Olivia hadn't been brought up with wealth, but what she did have was better than this.

"Lord, I'm looking at this all wrong, I know. You've provided for me all along in spite of myself. If, or I should say, when Olivia agrees to be my wife, You'll continue caring for us. And wherever we live, she'll bring her sweet touches with her." He continued his conversation with God until the coffee was ready.

Christmas was coming, and he had nothing to give Olivia. Maybe, just maybe, if this voyage was successful, he could pay a few bills current and buy her a ring.

Olivia wore a size six band. He'd measured one of her rings that she'd left on top of the shelf above her kitchen sink. The jeweler had assured him a ruby and diamond ring would be lovely for an engagement ring. Not the usual ring; but then Olivia wasn't a usual woman.

So much hinged on this upcoming fishing trip and on Olivia's change of heart. Jonathan shook his head and took his coffee outside onto the small porch. The air bit into him. Snow. He felt the dampness, though the sky was clear with thousands of stars twinkling above. They were due their first snowstorm of the year. He prayed the clear weather would hold.

* * *

"Frances, I'm wondering if the apartment above your shop is still empty." Olivia was sitting across from Frances at the Sea Dawg. The woman had accepted her invitation to lunch on Monday.

"Yes, as a matter of fact, it is. The last applicants backed out after they saw the tiny bathroom." Frances's new honey-colored hair made her appear years younger.

"Well, I'm interested. I could stop by the store for an application."

Frances smiled. "Nonsense. Forget an application. I'll even waive the security deposit. You were almost family once. That still counts to me."

"Thank you."

"It's crowded at home with two women, isn't it?" Frances took a bite of her seafood salad.

"Yeah. I'm thinking my parents need their space, and my original reason for coming home doesn't exist anymore. Dad doesn't need me to help him. He's got—" Olivia realized the word "Mom" nearly sprang from her lips as naturally as if she'd called Belinda Mom her whole life.

Frances nodded. "I know. It's time to let go. Like I should have been ready to let Robby go when he decided to marry you...." She frowned, the wrinkles deepening on her face.

"It's okay." Olivia squeezed Frances's hand. "You can visit me for coffee anytime you like."

They chatted about the apartment for a while longer, then Olivia decided to spend the afternoon Christmas shopping. She and Frances parted, promising to meet again to discuss her move-in date.

Christmas would be slim this year, but Olivia didn't mind. It was the first Christmas she'd be with her family. Her real family. Jonathan, she'd heard, was flying to Florida to see his parents. Maggie and Todd would be busy with their very special gift by then.

Belinda would appreciate some handcrafted jewelry. Olivia

stopped by Frances's shop and went to the display where Genevieve, a lady from church, sold some elegant pieces from estates as well as jewelry crafted by local artisans. She found a necklace and earring set that would match one of her mother's suits.

The noonday weather forecast caught Olivia's attention. One of the other employees had set the dial to the local station.

"It looks like snow is coming our way," the reporter announced. "Combined with a cold front crossing over Cape Cod, the Fairport area could receive anywhere from four to eight inches of snow, with higher amounts farther inland. But that's not all. Batten down the hatches for wind gusts up to fifty miles per hour." The announcer finished the forecast, cautioning boaters and Christmas shoppers alike.

"Brr, it already makes me feel colder!" Genevieve said as she arranged a display.

"I think the temperature's been dropping all day. I might stop shopping after this and just go home for the afternoon and write." Olivia touched an elegant ring, then set it down.

"I hope Jonathan and his guys are going to be okay."

Olivia turned her head to stare at Genevieve. "What?"

Genevieve's dark eyes rounded. "Oh, I thought you knew. Jonathan took his boat out for a run with the new engine. Jeremy mentioned to pray for him yesterday in Sunday school."

"I didn't know." She'd skipped Sunday school yesterday, and had instead joined her parents for breakfast.

"Well," Genevieve said as she wrapped Belinda's gift, "I'm sure Jonathan kept an eye on the forecast."

"Yes, I hope he did." But Olivia's stomach threatened to drop to her feet.

Chapter 19

Clouds were building up to the northwest, and the wind attacked the crew of the *Isabella Rose* with a vengeance. Jonathan kept an eye on the rapidly changing forecast. One more set of nets to pull in, and they would head for home. If the crew had become jittery, none of them let on. They were eager for a good haul and to return to their families.

The last look at Doppler radar had shown Jonathan there was plenty of time to return before the storm struck with its fury. By the time the snow fell, he'd be home again, warm and safe.

He listened to the rumbling engine doing its job below. *Thank You, Lord, for friends who care. And thank You for making my dream possible. Now see us home to safe harbor.*

"Everything okay, Jon?" Stumpy stuck his head into the pilothouse.

"Yeah, we're doing fine. Let's wrap this up quick, though. We've got some weather coming in." He followed the older man into the cold.

The boat gave a wild pitch. Stumpy's feet slid, and the man struck the deck's railing. His boots went over the side last.

"Stumpy!" Jonathan dashed to the side. He slammed into the railing. "Grab on!" He leaned over, extending a boat hook into the frothing water.

The other men rallied around; a pair of hands clamped onto Jonathan's waders, preventing him from joining Stumpy in the icy waves. *Lord, help!* What looked like a wall of angry black ocean headed straight for them.

Olivia jerked awake, sprawled on her bed. The late-afternoon twilight had come; she'd actually fallen asleep reading, despite her worry about Jonathan. But Todd had assured her Jonathan would be fine.

The delightful smells of her mother's corned beef and cabbage dinner reached Olivia's bedroom. Belinda had looked surprised when Olivia told her about the apartment. It was for the best, she reminded herself. Her parents didn't need her hanging around. Besides, she was an adult woman who needed a place of her own.

Jonathan. His face came to mind, the look she loved best, a day's worth of beard, black curly hair and snapping eyes.

"Protect him, Lord. Bring him home safe. Thank You for watching him even when I'm not there." Worry still niggled the pit of her stomach.

Looking at the snow falling outside, whipped around by the wind, didn't help either. Olivia yanked her curtains closed to block out the sight, and went to find safety in the warmth downstairs.

Belinda sat at the computer, entering figures and talking on her cell phone. "Yes, I know it's the holiday season. Well, see what you can work out. The Karwoskis want to start renovating the building by New Year's. I understand." She ended the call and faced Olivia. "Hey. Your father's on his way home from his radiation treatment."

"How's that? I didn't think we were letting him drive back and forth."

"Maggie had an OB appointment today, so she and Todd took him along to the medical center. They should be here any time now. Maybe they'll stay for supper." Belinda clicked on the mouse, and the figures disappeared.

"That sounds nice. I've missed seeing her lately." Olivia worried her lower lip with her top teeth.

"Are you doing okay?"

"I can't believe Jonathan did something so stupid." Olivia smacked a clenched fist on the desktop. "He knew the weather could turn, he knew there's not a big chance of bringing in a good haul. So why did he do it?" She paced the entryway.

Belinda sighed. "I honestly don't know. I never pretended to understand the compulsion these men have with the sea." A crease appeared on her forehead. "I need to check on supper." Belinda left her place at the computer and headed to the kitchen.

The front door opened behind Olivia. She turned. "Dad, how did it go?" Olivia hugged him and shivered from the cold air he brought inside.

"As well as usual. I'll be glad when I'm done with this. Hope I don't glow in the dark afterward. Todd's bringing Maggie in." Her father turned and held the door for Todd, whose arm was around Maggie's shoulders. Her stomach protruded from the front of her coat buttoned at the neck.

"Hey, Liv. It looks like we're going to stay here for a while. Maggie's dilated to three centimeters, so the doctor told us to wait it out until her contractions get closer together." Todd took the coat from his wife's shoulders.

"Of course you will. Our house is closer to the medical center than yours is out on that shoreline. The roads are probably getting slick anyway. We'll have a slumber party. Sort of." Olivia noted the pained look on Maggie's face. "Maggie, go ahead and sit down. Dad might even give up his easy chair for you."

"I don't feel like sitting down." Maggie's features softened. "Sorry. I've been getting twinges ever since my exam. And I didn't want to be cooped up at the hospital all day."

Todd was busily punching numbers on his cell phone. His face blanched while he listened to his messages. "Liv."

"What is it?" She shouldn't have asked, didn't want to hear what came next.

"I had a message from the harbormaster's office. They lost contact with Jonathan's boat over an hour ago."

Jonathan felt the icy tentacles of fear wrapping around his entire being. The cold of the ocean was nothing compared to this bitter feeling.

The boat had righted itself after rolling with the impact of a waterwall. Unfortunately, the radar and satellite antennas had snapped off with the force of the pressure. Jeff kept trying to get a signal with his digital phone to call Todd.

Only survival mattered now.

After they'd rescued Stumpy from the water, they collectively decided to make a run for home. Jonathan had noted their heading, which pointed to Fairport. Now they had just a compass to guide them.

It would be easier to give in, to allow the wind and the waves to batter them until the storm gave out.

Head for home, head for home, head for home repeated urgently in his head. He gripped the helm, feeling the power of the water trying to rip control of the boat from his hands. *Lord, You are the Master of the sea. I commit the rest of this voyage to You.*

Olivia would be frantic. Jonathan's thoughts were with her, wherever she was.

The corn beef chased the cabbage around Olivia's plate several times before she gave up on eating. She joined Maggie in the living room, where her friend sat hugging a pillow.

"How are you?" Olivia watched Maggie breathe through a contraction.

"I'm fine. Sort of." Maggie relaxed her hold on the pillow. "But I could ask you the same question."

"I'm ready to pace the house if it would help." Olivia tried to put a brave smile on her face. "I can't believe Todd let you leave the hospital."

"I'm more relaxed here. If need be, it's a close drive to the medical center. Your dad was a sweetheart to give up his recliner." Maggie reached for her cup of ice. "The smell of that food is killing me. Wish I could eat something!"

"I wish I could, too. Oh, it's six now. Turn on the news for Dad." Olivia sat back, knowing the storm would be a highlight of the local news.

Native New Englanders dealt with and lived through weather rather than feared it. Olivia knew one winter storm wasn't a big deal. Out on the water, though, it was a different story.

"Tonight, a nor'easter barrels down from Canada, bringing plenty of wind and snow. A cold front has stalled over Cape Cod, holding the Massachusetts coast in an icy grip with the two fronts. More after the headlines." The news anchor went on to talk about holiday sales figures and other matters that Olivia tuned out. What she really wanted to do was find out more about Jonathan's heading, where he was when they lost contact with him. While the rest of the world thought about presents and holiday activities, Olivia focused on one fishing boat somewhere off the coast.

She could ask Todd, but she knew his concern was focused on Maggie and the upcoming arrival of the baby.

Todd settled onto the love seat with a cup of coffee. He held his cell phone in one hand, his thumb nimbly tapping the number keys. "That's strange."

"What's that, honey?" Maggie said through clenched teeth.

"Somebody called and didn't leave a message, but I don't know the number. And all I hear on the voice mail is static."

"Todd, where did the harbormaster say they lost touch with Jonathan?"

"About fifty miles out, just offshore."

Olivia sighed. Fifty miles. In good weather, the trip would take them hours. Tonight, their return would be nothing short of a nightmare voyage.

She sat up when she heard the weather forecast. "Tonight, the coastal waves will be eight to ten feet, with possibly double the size further from shore. It's not a night for sailing," the meteorologist joked.

"Waves up to twenty feet offshore?" Olivia went for her coat, scarf and gloves. "I'm going out for a while."

"No! The roads are getting worse," her father called out.

"I'll be fine. Where are my gloves?" Olivia fumbled around the entryway shelf. She'd left them upstairs. Taking the steps two at a time, she nearly collided with Belinda at the top of the stairs.

"Did you hear something? Where are you going?" Belinda held her by the elbows.

"Out." Olivia stood back. "I'll be careful. I've got my phone."

She left before anyone talked her out of it. The cold night surrounded her, snow stinging her face. Olivia brushed two inches of snow from her car's windshield. Not too bad so far. Just the wind that clawed and tore at her until she shut the car door.

Olivia let the engine idle until the defroster starting doing its job. Where was she going? She didn't want to drive and wander too far, then get stuck somewhere. Downtown seemed the best idea.

The car brought her to the waterfront on Western Avenue, to the statue of the Fisherman of Fairport. She parked the car and let it idle. The monument stood in the feeble glow of the streetlamps, lighting up the snow whipping across the little plaza. Olivia could quote the verse gracing the monument. "They that go down to the sea in ships." She reached for her

Bible that she'd left in the car from Sunday service, and turned the pages to Psalm 107.

She kept reading. "Who do business on great waters, they see the wonders of the Lord, and His wonders of the deep. For He commands and raises the stormy wind, which lifts up the waves of the sea. They mount up to the heavens, they go down again to the depths; their soul melts because of trouble.

"They reel to and fro, and stagger like a drunken man, and are at their wits' end. Then they cry out to the Lord in their trouble, and He brings them out of their distresses.

"He calms the storm, so that its waves are still. Then they are glad because they are quiet; so He guides them to their desired haven."

The windshield wipers kept up their relentless *swish-swish, swish-swish*. Olivia leaned her head back against the headrest. Was Jonathan reeling to and fro, like the ones in the psalm? There was nothing she could do except wait and pray.

Outside, the storm's wildness beckoned, wind gusts tapping the car as if daring Olivia to venture into the gale. She turned off the ignition, tucked her keys into her purse and reached for her Bible. No storm would keep her huddled in a car.

She stepped onto the snowy road, securing her car and noticing that the weekday traffic had dwindled. On any normal night, the good citizens would be traveling home and stopping off at the market for this or that. Except tonight, Olivia realized as she trudged to the circular plaza where the statue stood and faced the open water.

Where was Jonathan? And why did the fear rise up with every wave that battered the edges of the harbor? The inky waters swallowed up the innocence of the driving white snow.

"I can do this!" The wind carried her shout away as she walked onto the harborfront pier. "I'm stronger now, God, I am!"

Yet she had come full circle and still felt no different. A man she loved was in peril. Her best friend needed her, and here she stood at the harbor, wrestling with a situation over which she had no control.

Olivia sank onto a snow-covered bench and bowed her head. "I'm foolish and I'm weak. That's it. I'm not in control." She looked up at the figure of the fisherman. "I couldn't help Maggie, couldn't save Robby, couldn't keep Dad from getting sick…couldn't keep Mom from leaving us." The tears chilled on her cheeks. "And I can't save Jonathan now."

She shivered despite her long wool coat, the cold seeming to penetrate to her soul. "Mom was right. Frances was right. I can't control many of the things or people in my life."

She had decided to follow God when she was a young child, and all along the way she had yanked the reins of her life from Him, or tried to, whenever it was convenient or things looked too scary.

The wind flapped the pages of her Bible, not allowing her gloved fingers to find the verse that came to mind. Something about the Lord caring for His people like a shepherd tends his sheep. He loved them and protected them.

"I've been wrong." Olivia wasn't sure if she was praying or talking to herself. Maybe she'd better sit in the car. Even if no one saw her, at least she could read in relative comfort.

Only when she saw her purse on the front seat of her locked car did she realize her mistake.

"Get that other pump going!" Jonathan shouted across the hold at Freddy, who closed the casing on the pump. The bilge pump Jonathan was working on was refusing to cooperate. If they went into a barrel roll and took on too much water, the ship wouldn't right herself again. And then the *Isabella Rose* would join the *Lady Jane* at her final resting place. The inflatable raft would be battered in these seas and useless.

He heard noises from above. Stumpy had the helm. Jeff was shouting into the cell phone. "I think I'm getting through! Hang on down there!"

Jonathan tried to respond, but his work on the pump was

rewarded when the pump roared to life. The ceiling turned into the floor, and Jonathan crashed to the other side of the hold.

"Look out!"

A rush of water swept through the hold. Jonathan lost his footing. A searing crack of pain reverberated in his skull. Nausea came as he saw blood mingling with the seawater. Then the roaring began in his ears and his vision went fuzzy.

Olivia… Jonathan barely felt the splash as his body hit the shallow water.

Chapter 20

Olivia slammed her fist on the roof of her car. Of all the times to lock herself out of her own car. There lay her purse with the car keys inside, cell phone on the seat.

"Great, I get it." She looked at the snow-swirled sky. "Yet another way You remind me I'm not in charge. I guess You've got me stuck here for a reason." Olivia shook her head. She tucked her Bible under one arm and slipped her wool scarf over her head.

She could walk to the nearest open business and call her family to see if someone could bring her spare keys. While her boots crunched a steady rhythm as they carried her through the snow, a tune came to mind. *...little ones to Him belong, they are weak but He is strong...Yes, Jesus loves me, yes, Jesus loves me...the Bible tells me so.*

Olivia stopped. Jesus was strong enough for her. She didn't have to try. *Who can separate us from the love of God?*

"You love me!" She hugged the Bible tighter. "No matter what happens, no matter how weak I feel...You're taking care of everything…You've always been taking care of everything." The lights across the harbor twinkled through the snowfall. "Even when I was little, and Mom was gone. And Dad would leave on his fishing trips. Then when I lost Robby no matter how tightly I tried to hold him. When Dad was sick. And even tonight."

Olivia marched to the railing at the memorial. "You know how frightened I've been, how worried I am. But I know You're with Jonathan even now. And You love him, too, so much more than I could ever try to love him." Her hand felt the cold metal through the glove. "No matter what happens."

She looked at the Bible she held in the crook of her arm. "Please help me to remember Your love above all else. If I remember Your love, I know that Your control is like a loving hand carrying me…."

The storm raged on around her, yet inside it felt as if a balm applied itself to her heart and drove away the cold. Even though she stood at the edge of the cliff, she knew who held her hand.

"Thank You for keeping me here long enough to hear You." Olivia shivered. "Thank You for loving Jonathan, too. I won't say I'm not worried about him, but I know You're working even if I don't feel it." Trust, simple trust, not based on feelings.

It was time to go home. Her family waited for her. And she needed to wait for Jonathan.

"Honey, we were so worried." Her mother embraced her before she handed Olivia a mug of hot chocolate. "I tried calling and you didn't answer. Maggie's at the hospital now. Her contractions came faster and faster. I imagine they'll have a new little one sometime tonight."

"I can't wait to hear!" Olivia sipped the cocoa. "But I have to tell you some things."

"Oh?"

"You were right." Finally, she felt like she was beginning

to thaw out in more ways than one. "I thought if I took care of things myself, I could keep everyone safe. I really didn't think God was doing His job all that well." Her throat caught.

Her mother sniffed and dabbed at her own eyes. "In spite of me, He took care of you. I'm so proud of you."

"I love you, Mom."

The two women embraced. Old anger had been washed away.

The phone call from Todd came at the coldest hour of the night when Olivia had finally dozed in her father's chair.

"Is it Maggie?" Olivia's mouth felt plugged with cotton.

"No, she's still in labor." His pause made Olivia's stomach retie itself in a knot. "It's Jonathan."

"What happened? Where is he?"

"He's just been brought unconscious into the E.R., except—"

"I'm on my way!" She slammed down the phone. Still dressed in her sweats, she yanked on her coat, then scribbled a note for her parents.

"I will not be afraid. I'm in God's loving care, no matter what happens." She locked the door behind her. "No matter how I feel."

Olivia crunched through the snow to her car, did a cursory scraping of the windshield and set out. She felt the love surging to her fingertips so much that she expected it to pop through the fingers of her gloves that gripped the cold steering wheel.

The rear end of the car fishtailed as she turned onto Atlantic Avenue and headed for the hospital. Olivia's foot automatically lifted from the accelerator; she turned the wheel and allowed the car to straighten.

Jonathan needed her. She would be there for him, always.

Jonathan's head roared as he lay on the stretcher in the E.R. The hospital staff worked on him, shining lights in his eyes. Someone shouted something about a head scan. His lungs burned. Every breath caused tingling pain and there didn't seem to be enough air. He reached for the source of the pain in his head.

"Don't touch. I'm going to suture this laceration," a stern yet calming male voice admonished him. "I'm Dr. Caproni. You're in the Fairport E.R. You've got a pretty nasty gash on your head, a possible concussion and you've swallowed a lot of water."

The voice went on to ask him questions about himself, the day of the week and the year and the name of the president. All Jonathan wanted was sleep or relief from the pressure building in his head. The blackness beckoned to him.

"Hang on. Peterson, epinephrine, stat!"

He was so tired. Olivia…

Olivia nearly collided with a nurse as she burst through the doors of the E.R. She paused, forcing herself to take a deep breath. They'd probably want to medicate her if she pounced on the desk like a wild woman.

She approached the clerk at the information desk. "Excuse me, I'm looking for Jonathan Barrotta. He's just arrived here."

"Are you family?" The tired-looking woman shuffled through some papers.

"No, I'm not family." Olivia's hopes sank.

"I'm sorry. I can't tell you any more. Confidentiality and regulations…" The woman smiled sympathetically.

Olivia sighed. "Thank you anyway. But please, if you can get him a message, let him know I'm here." She might as well head for Labor and Delivery to see about Maggie. And maybe she'd find someone to tell her something about Jonathan.

She trudged to the maternity floor, her boots seeming to grow heavier with every step. Todd was standing in the waiting room, talking to Maggie's parents and grinning.

"Todd, how is she?" Olivia felt her lips forming a smile, then corrected herself. "How are they?"

He removed the green scrubs he wore. "Both Maggie and

Lydia are doing wonderfully." Todd's eyes were red, his face split into a wide grin. "It's a miracle."

She hugged him, and congratulated Maggie's parents. "I can't wait to see them both." She was dying to ask him about Jonathan, what else he knew, but didn't want to squelch their joyful moment.

"She's perfect. She's beautiful." Todd released a chuckle. "Aw, I can't wait to take more pictures."

Maggie's parents left the room to see their daughter. Todd assured them he'd follow. When he turned back to face Olivia, she could see fresh worry on his face.

"What is it? What happened to Jonathan?"

Todd led her to a chair. "The *Isabella Rose* made it home, but just barely. One of the guys called me. He was the one who called earlier. Anyway, Jonathan was injured while working on the bilge pumps. They nearly lost him and Freddy, the hold had filled with enough water…and he's got a bad gash on his head, lost a lot of blood."

Olivia clamped a hand on her mouth and groaned. She removed her hand to speak. "But he's alive. I wish I could see him. Do his parents know?"

Todd nodded. "I called them in Florida. They're flying out as soon as they can get a flight to Logan." He put a hand on her shoulder. "The one doctor I spoke with said Jonathan's got a lot of pressure building up in his brain." Evidently Todd had had better success gaining information.

"So that's why they're operating. The clerk downstairs wouldn't tell me anything…." Olivia rubbed her chilled fingers together.

"Let's pray for him real quick." Todd's grin came back. "And then I'll sneak you in to see Maggie." They bowed their heads and prayed for skill for the doctors and Jonathan's recovery.

Olivia followed Todd to a semiprivate room, where an exhausted yet radiant Maggie held a wrinkled infant on her chest. Her eyes glittered with tears that ran down her face.

"Mag…" Olivia's throat caught at the sight of the little bundle. Now was not a time to storm the operating room and demand what was being done for the man she loved. Now was a time to rejoice with her friends.

"I never thought I'd be so tired or hurt so bad," Maggie said. "But she's worth it. Oh, yes, she's worth it." Her gaze drifted up to Todd.

Olivia slipped off her coat and settled onto the chair by the bed. "I'm so happy for you. So glad. I should have brought you something, but I was kind of in a hurry…."

Maggie nodded. "Todd just told me. Hey, it's going to be all right." She reached over the bed railing for Olivia's hand.

"I know." Olivia's throat caught again. "May I hold her?"

"Sure, but wash your hands…." Maggie gestured at the sink with her head.

Olivia complied and took the featherlight newborn into the crook of her left arm. A sweet rush of joy swept through her. Little Lydia stirred; a tiny fist went to a petal pink mouth.

A new life had appeared tonight in the world. Olivia's heart rejoiced for Maggie and Todd. "She's an answer to prayer, isn't she?" Soft laughter bubbled up inside her. The jiggling caused Lydia's eyelids to flutter. "Oopsy. Hope she's not going to squall yet!"

"So Aunt Olivia, is your life going to be different now?" Maggie teased. "You look quite a bit more peaceful than when I saw you leave the house tonight."

Olivia placed Lydia back in Maggie's arms. "Yes, I hope so. I'm here to see you, but for Jonathan, too. There's so much I have to tell him."

Todd frowned. He took his place at Maggie's side and reached a finger down to stroke his little daughter's cheek. "I pray he's willing to listen and doesn't get pigheaded."

"What are you talking about?" Olivia tried to keep her voice even.

"From what it sounds like, the *Isabella* might not be seaworthy again or worth repairing." Todd's eyes met hers; disappointment filled his expression. "Jonathan's sunk everything he's got into this boat. I hope his pride doesn't get the better of him."

The angry water poured into the hold, black as ink, threatening to swallow Jonathan up. His arms and legs felt pinned to the floor—or was he on the ceiling? Was the outside water filling the compartments, forcing out the oxygen and sending them all to the bottom of the ocean?

He heard a soft voice above the crashing waves. Olivia? Something about everything being all right, that God was with him and carrying him. But something still felt wrong.

A pounding in his head like a jackhammer greeted Jonathan as he fought his way to consciousness. Warm, strong hands gripped one of his. He could smell flowers. No, perfume. Olivia's. He wished his hands would cooperate.

"So you see, it doesn't matter to me what you do, Jon. I love you.... I love you...." A gulp silenced her voice.

His eyes focused on her face, etched with concern, her eyes fixed on his chapped hands. He tried to speak, but his throat throbbed. Olivia's gaze flicked to his face.

"Oh, you're awake! I was hoping you'd hear me. I begged one of the nurses to let me sit with you, because your mom and dad aren't here yet. And Maggie had her baby." A blush colored her face while she babbled.

His parents were coming. Jonathan closed his eyes. Now his failure would be complete, and all would see him for what he really was.

Olivia kept chattering about the baby, her name and something about going walking at the harbor during the storm and then locking her keys in her car. Part of him wanted to laugh, listening to her mouth motor away nonstop. This was the Olivia he loved. A sparkle flared up in her eyes when she touched his cheek.

"There's so much I have to explain. I've been up almost all night, and I know you've just had surgery, but I had to stay here and at least talk." She stood up, then leaned over him. "I'm glad you're home."

Her lips were soft on his face, the best thing he'd felt in a long time. Their whisper-soft touch caressed his forehead, cheeks, then found his mouth. They lingered; equally soft hands rested on his stubbled jaw. Jonathan wanted to slip an arm around her, but it wouldn't cooperate.

Olivia drew back. When she spoke, her voice sounded husky and low. "Welcome home, my love. I'll always be here for you. But right now I'll go get one of the nurses." She swept out to the hall.

Jonathan cleared his throat and fought off the edges of oblivion that threatened his senses. A nurse returned and noted his vital signs, and before she left, admonished Olivia to let Jonathan get some sleep. Olivia bobbed her head and stood to one corner of the room, and murmured something about sleeping in the chair.

"Liv," he managed to croak.

"Yes?" She was back at his side in a flash.

"Don't waste your time with me." The words stabbed him as he spoke.

"What are you talking about?"

"I've got nothing now. The *Isabella* is pretty much foundered; it's a miracle we made it back. And I've been a fool. You don't need this life, or someone like me in yours." He hated to see the agony cross her face. Yet he knew he spoke the truth. "Go home, sleep. Everything will be okay." He closed his eyes, hating himself for the pain he'd just inflicted.

Olivia watched Jonathan succumb to much-needed sleep. He couldn't have meant what he'd just said. Maybe it was the medication. Although Todd had mentioned something earlier about male pride. *Stubborn, pigheaded...*

But she didn't care. She situated herself in the chair by the bed, accepted the blanket and neck pillow from the nurse, and allowed herself to doze. She'd show him she wouldn't run off. Not this time.

By the time morning came, every muscle in Olivia's neck and back screamed from being in the chair. Jonathan still slept. A nurse would come through, note his vital signs, then leave. One even gave Olivia a sad smile.

The Barrottas arrived from Florida not long after lunch. Olivia found them in Jonathan's room after she'd left to grab a bite and call home to tell her parents about Jonathan.

"Olivia, it's good to see you again. Not in this way, though." Janet Barrotta, an elegant-looking woman with graying hair, embraced her. "I'm glad Jon's got you."

"Thanks. He tried to drive me off earlier, but I'm not budging."

Tom Barrotta shook his head. "Stubborn boy. He told me he'd sunk everything into that boat."

Olivia bit her lip. "I know he's disappointed. But he tried. He tried very hard. And I'm proud of him." She squared her shoulders.

"He did try." Mr. Barrotta looked tired.

"And he doesn't have nothing." Olivia nodded. "He's talented, hardworking and has a faith in God that teaches me lessons. No, he has a lot."

Mrs. Barrotta patted Olivia's arm. "And you love him, don't you?"

"Yes, I do. No matter what." She gave half a smile, then yawned. "I'm sorry. I want to be here when he wakes up, but I'm so tired."

"Go ahead home. Give me your number and I'll call you when Jonathan wakes."

Olivia gave Mrs. Barrotta her cell number. She yawned once more. She'd go home to sleep and prepare to show Jonathan she'd be there for him.

Chapter 21

Jonathan could finally sit up two mornings later without waves of nausea racking his body. He begged off the promethazine injections, refusing to feel drugged. The pain medication did that enough.

He didn't want to think about the medical bills. Hopefully, they'd let him go home that afternoon. According to the doctor, they'd had to relieve the pressure and swelling in his skull. Aside from some bruises and the gash in his forehead and the concussion, he felt fine.

And aside from his heart, now that he'd told Olivia to go on without him.

Jonathan fingered the phone numbers on the scrap of paper his mother had left. He'd begged her not to call Olivia.

His Bible sat on the tray next to his untouched breakfast. Jonathan knew he needed both, but right now he let them be.

He needed to call his insurance company and make an appointment for a claims adjuster to assess his boat. Maybe he'd be able to pay off his debts and the hospital bills. Then he'd figure out what to do next.

"Lord, I'm sorry. I'm not what Olivia needs. I'm no provider for her. I couldn't hack it. And now, no one in town will ship out with me." He studied one of the 144 tiles in the ceiling. "Plus, I was wrong. I thought it was Your will for me to have a boat and to fish. How can I expect to know Your will for me and for Olivia? And if we had kids—" Jonathan refused thoughts of a future and a family at the moment.

A hard rap sounded in the doorway. Sam entered the room.

"I came to talk some sense into you."

"How did you get in?" Jonathan craned his neck to see into the hallway.

"Through the front door." Sam crossed his arms in front of him.

"No one but family or my pastor was supposed to be allowed to visit."

"I told them I was your future father-in-law."

"Aw, Sam."

"My Liv's wondering why you haven't called her and won't let her visit you. Nobody treats my baby girl like that. I don't care if you are in a hospital bed." The man's eyes flashed.

"It's for the best. I can't provide for her. I don't have anything." Jonathan clenched his jaw.

With two strides, Sam crossed the room and grabbed Jonathan's hands. His viselike grip squeezed tighter and tighter. "You've got these two hands. Hardworking hands." The man released one of his hands and gave Jonathan's chest a nudge. "And your heart." Then he tapped the bandage on Jonathan's forehead. "And a good head on your shoulders, even though it's about the hardest one I've seen."

Jonathan clenched his free hand into a fist. "She deserves better."

"She deserves you." Sam released Jonathan's hand from his grip, and Jonathan tried not to flex his fingers in relief. "Besides, isn't your God big enough?"

"What?"

"Don't look so shocked. I'm not a churchgoing man, at least I wasn't until recently. But if God is as big as you say and as powerful, wouldn't He take good care of you two?" Sam shook his head. "Boy, but you do have a hard head!" Sam strode to the window and studied the bright winter day outside.

If I've ever been wrong, Lord, it's now. And having a man who hasn't been to church in years to teach me a lesson. Forgive my pride. The knowledge of what he'd done to Olivia pained him.

"I'm sorry."

Sam whirled from where he stood. "That's a start."

"I've had so much pride, worrying about my image. What others thought about me. You know how those guys are, Sam." Jonathan swallowed hard; at least it didn't hurt so much to talk anymore. "I've been wrong. Do you think she'll come if I ask her to?"

"Like a shot." Sam grinned for the first time since he'd walked into the hospital room. "But before you call her, I've got a business proposition for you. See, Lindy doesn't mind me lobstering. Lindy says I could get a website and sell my lobsters direct. Except I'll need help. So I've been thinking about taking on a partner. Are you interested?"

Jonathan felt hope blooming inside. "Let's talk."

"What has Dad gone and done now?" Olivia demanded of her mother. She'd taken advantage of her father leaving the house to wrap his Christmas gifts.

"He said he'd had enough of you moping around the house. So I think he went to pound some sense into Jonathan." Her mother looked up from her laptop at the kitchen table.

"Oh, no!" Surely he hadn't. "Why did he do that? When did he leave?"

"A few hours ago. Then he said he had to go to the bank, then to the Sea Dawg to meet some of the guys for lunch. But you know your dad. Nobody makes his little girl cry." Her mother smiled, then rested her chin on her hand. "It's going to work out. I know it."

Olivia shifted from her knees and sat cross-legged on the living room floor. "I saw the *Isabella Rose* in the harbor. She looks awful. I don't see how he'll get her fit to ship out with again."

"I sure hope your dad didn't lose his temper."

"You don't think?" Olivia's heart started to pound faster. "I've got to go apologize. Who knows what Dad's gone and said to Jonathan."

She left her father's present half-wrapped on the floor and went straight to the hospital. She found Jonathan's room empty.

A nurse met her in the doorway. "He's been discharged home. Against doctor's orders..."

"Thanks." Olivia dashed for the elevator.

What had her father said? Or worse, done? She needed to face Jonathan, to explain she hadn't sent her father to talk to him.

She parked at Jonathan's apartment and bounded up the porch stairs.

Jonathan answered the door. "Hi..." He looked less pale than she remembered and he'd shaved. One arm was in a sling and his head was bandaged. It was all she could do to keep from rushing to him.

"Please don't send me away." Olivia could barely breathe. "I need to explain. My dad..."

A smile covered his face, the grin she'd never grow tired of seeing. "You don't have to explain. And I'm not letting you get away. Not if I can help it." He reached for her with his free hand and pulled her inside the warm apartment.

"It all came down to trust." Olivia let him lead her into his living room, where he pulled her down to sit next to him on the couch. "I didn't trust God, not really. I thought I could run my life, especially if it seemed like God wasn't cooperating. Or if I got disappointed."

Jonathan wore an amused expression on his face, but said nothing.

She let herself continue. "The other night out at the harbor, I realized it's God's love that carries us through everything. He cares for you so much more than I could. And I've been wrong, trying to do His job for Him. I mean—"

He put a finger on her lips.

"What?" she mumbled.

"Shh, you talk too much." Then he kissed her until she was breathless and forgot what she'd been trying to explain.

"It's my turn now." Jonathan kissed the end of her nose, and she attempted not to giggle, her mind still trying to comprehend what had happened. "I was full of pride, thinking I had nothing to offer you. I'm so sorry I hurt you. I have nothing right now. Except this." He fished a velvet box from under the cushion.

"What?" she repeated, realizing what he was showing her. When did he get a ring?

"My parents gave it to me. It's a family ring they've had in a safe-deposit box until the right time." The antique setting displayed a stunning diamond that winked at her as if it knew a secret. Olivia let her mouth hang open while Jonathan slid the ring onto her finger. "Marry me."

Olivia nodded. "Of course I will." She touched his face, relishing the thought of waking up with him every morning, of the children to come, of the life that lay ahead. "I love you."

He pulled her close and kissed her again.

Epilogue

The warm June wind teased the edges of Olivia's veil. She reached a hand up to pull it down. Her other hand clutched her bouquet and was tucked around her father's arm as they walked along the path toward the ocean. Violin and cello mingled with the sounds of the surf.

"Did I tell you you're beautiful?"

"No, Dad."

"Well, you are. You remind me of my Lindy." He raised her veil and kissed her cheek.

The leftover chill from the night before lingered in the sand that sifted between Olivia's bare feet, but it didn't matter to her. Jonathan waited for her on "their" beach, along with friends and family who'd come to witness their vows. Over the winter months that followed Jonathan's recovery, they had spent many hours walking the beach, and decided to share the spot of beauty with their wedding guests.

Olivia's throat ached when they reached the edge of the dunes, and she caught sight of the display before them. Rows of white chairs faced the water, a white runner dividing them like an aisle. At the very end stood Jonathan, barefooted but in a tuxedo.

Her mother and Maggie stood, holding bouquets of lilies, across from Todd and Jeremy. Maggie held Lydia on one hip.

Then after the glorious music, her father entrusted her to Jonathan's care. She would love this man all her days. Whatever came their way, the love of their Heavenly Father would sustain them.

After uttering the sweet sacred words that bound them together, Jonathan and Olivia shared a kiss. Then the icy water swirled over her toes, and Olivia squealed, gathering her skirts and pulling Jonathan away from the water.

She saw her parents laughing, her mother snapping pictures. The candid shots would be a treasured part of their album.

Jonathan kissed Olivia again. "I can't wait to get you to the cottage in Maine."

Belinda laid a hand on Olivia's arm. "Wait. You remember I said I'd get permission from the landowner to have the ceremony here?"

Olivia nodded. She'd appreciated her mother's help with the wedding without too much of a power struggle between them.

"Well, I did better than that." She pressed an envelope into Olivia's hands. "Before you say anything, just consider this a wedding gift. And more birthday and Christmas gifts and 'I love you' gifts than I want to count."

"Mom…" Olivia handed her bouquet to Jonathan and opened the envelope. It was a deed for two acres of shoreline property.

"Please. You two can have fun planning your house and building it here. You won't be in Frances O'Leary's apartment forever." Her mother blinked and dabbed at her eyes.

"Oh, phooey, my mascara's already mussed." She laughed. "Just build your house with love."

Olivia looked up into Jonathan's eyes. "We will, Mom. You can count on it."

* * * * *

REQUEST YOUR FREE BOOKS!

2 FREE INSPIRATIONAL NOVELS
PLUS 2
FREE
MYSTERY GIFTS

Love Inspired

YES! Please send me 2 FREE Love Inspired® novels and my 2 FREE mystery gifts (gifts are worth about $10). After receiving them, if I don't wish to receive any more books, I can return the shipping statement marked "cancel." If I don't cancel, I will receive 6 brand-new novels every month and be billed just $4.74 per book in the U.S. or $5.24 per book in Canada. That's a savings of at least 21% off the cover price. It's quite a bargain! Shipping and handling is just 50¢ per book in the U.S. and 75¢ per book in Canada.* I understand that accepting the 2 free books and gifts places me under no obligation to buy anything. I can always return a shipment and cancel at any time. Even if I never buy another book, the two free books and gifts are mine to keep forever.

105/305 IDN F49N

Name   (PLEASE PRINT)

Address   Apt. #

City   State/Prov.   Zip/Postal Code

Signature (if under 18, a parent or guardian must sign)

Mail to the **Harlequin® Reader Service:**
IN U.S.A.: P.O. Box 1867, Buffalo, NY 14240-1867
IN CANADA: P.O. Box 609, Fort Erie, Ontario L2A 5X3

**Are you a subscriber to Love Inspired books
and want to receive the larger-print edition?
Call 1-800-873-8635 or visit www.ReaderService.com.**

* Terms and prices subject to change without notice. Prices do not include applicable taxes. Sales tax applicable in N.Y. Canadian residents will be charged applicable taxes. Offer not valid in Quebec. This offer is limited to one order per household. Not valid for current subscribers to Love Inspired books. All orders subject to credit approval. Credit or debit balances in a customer's account(s) may be offset by any other outstanding balance owed by or to the customer. Please allow 4 to 6 weeks for delivery. Offer available while quantities last.

Your Privacy—The Harlequin® Reader Service is committed to protecting your privacy. Our Privacy Policy is available online at www.ReaderService.com or upon request from the Harlequin Reader Service.
We make a portion of our mailing list available to reputable third parties that offer products we believe may interest you. If you prefer that we not exchange your name with third parties, or if you wish to clarify or modify your communication preferences, please visit us at www.ReaderService.com/consumerschoice or write to us at Harlequin Reader Service Preference Service, P.O. Box 9062, Buffalo, NY 14269. Include your complete name and address.

LIDIR13R

REQUEST YOUR FREE BOOKS!
2 FREE RIVETING INSPIRATIONAL NOVELS
PLUS 2 FREE MYSTERY GIFTS

YES! Please send me 2 FREE Love Inspired® Suspense novels and my 2 FREE mystery gifts (gifts are worth about $10). After receiving them, if I don't wish to receive any more books, I can return the shipping statement marked "cancel." If I don't cancel, I will receive 4 brand-new novels every month and be billed just $4.74 per book in the U.S. or $5.24 per book in Canada. That's a savings of at least 21% off the cover price. It's quite a bargain! Shipping and handling is just 50¢ per book in the U.S. and 75¢ per book in Canada.* I understand that accepting the 2 free books and gifts places me under no obligation to buy anything. I can always return a shipment and cancel at any time. Even if I never buy another book, the two free books and gifts are mine to keep forever.

123/323 IDN F5AN

Name	(PLEASE PRINT)	

Address		Apt. #

City	State/Prov.	Zip/Postal Code

Signature (if under 18, a parent or guardian must sign)

Mail to the **Harlequin® Reader Service:**
IN U.S.A.: P.O. Box 1867, Buffalo, NY 14240-1867
IN CANADA: P.O. Box 609, Fort Erie, Ontario L2A 5X3

**Are you a current subscriber to Love Inspired Suspense books and want to receive the larger-print edition?
Call 1-800-873-8635 or visit www.ReaderService.com.**

* Terms and prices subject to change without notice. Prices do not include applicable taxes. Sales tax applicable in N.Y. Canadian residents will be charged applicable taxes. Offer not valid in Quebec. This offer is limited to one order per household. Not valid for current subscribers to Love Inspired Suspense books. All orders subject to credit approval. Credit or debit balances in a customer's account(s) may be offset by any other outstanding balance owed by or to the customer. Please allow 4 to 6 weeks for delivery. Offer available while quantities last.

Your Privacy—The Harlequin® Reader Service is committed to protecting your privacy. Our Privacy Policy is available online at www.ReaderService.com or upon request from the Harlequin Reader Service.
We make a portion of our mailing list available to reputable third parties that offer products we believe may interest you. If you prefer that we not exchange your name with third parties, or if you wish to clarify or modify your communication preferences, please visit us at www.ReaderService.com/consumerschoice or write to us at Harlequin Reader Service Preference Service, P.O. Box 9062, Buffalo, NY 14269. Include your complete name and address.

LISDIR13R

REQUEST YOUR FREE BOOKS!

2 FREE INSPIRATIONAL NOVELS
PLUS 2
FREE
MYSTERY GIFTS

Love Inspired
HISTORICAL
INSPIRATIONAL HISTORICAL ROMANCE

YES! Please send me 2 FREE Love Inspired® Historical novels and my 2 FREE mystery gifts (gifts are worth about $10). After receiving them, if I don't wish to receive any more books, I can return the shipping statement marked "cancel." If I don't cancel, I will receive 4 brand-new novels every month and be billed just $4.74 per book in the U.S. or $5.24 per book in Canada. That's a savings of at least 21% off the cover price. It's quite a bargain! Shipping and handling is just 50¢ per book in the U.S. and 75¢ per book in Canada.* I understand that accepting the 2 free books and gifts places me under no obligation to buy anything. I can always return a shipment and cancel at any time. Even if I never buy another book, the two free books and gifts are mine to keep forever.

102/302 IDN F5CY

Name	(PLEASE PRINT)	
Address		Apt. #
City	State/Prov.	Zip/Postal Code

Signature (if under 18, a parent or guardian must sign)

Mail to the Harlequin® Reader Service:
IN U.S.A.: P.O. Box 1867, Buffalo, NY 14240-1867
IN CANADA: P.O. Box 609, Fort Erie, Ontario L2A 5X3

Want to try two free books from another series?
Call 1-800-873-8635 or visit www.ReaderService.com.

* Terms and prices subject to change without notice. Prices do not include applicable taxes. Sales tax applicable in N.Y. Canadian residents will be charged applicable taxes. Offer not valid in Quebec. This offer is limited to one order per household. Not valid for current subscribers to Love Inspired Historical books. All orders subject to credit approval. Credit or debit balances in a customer's account(s) may be offset by any other outstanding balance owed by or to the customer. Please allow 4 to 6 weeks for delivery. Offer available while quantities last.

LIHDIR13R

Reader Service.com

Manage your account online!

- Review your order history
- Manage your payments
- Update your address

*We've designed
the Harlequin® Reader Service
website just for you.*

Enjoy all the features!

- Reader excerpts from any series
- Respond to mailings and
  special monthly offers
- Discover new series available to you
- Browse the Bonus Bucks catalog
- Share your feedback

Visit us at:
ReaderService.com

RS13